PENGUIN CRIME FICTION

DEATH HAS GREEN FINGERS

Lionel Black was also Dudley Barker, a well-known author, broadcaster, and journalist in England. After coming down from Oxford, he worked in most capacities on newspaper editorial staffs in London and the provinces, including long periods with the London *Evening Standard* and the London *Daily Herald*. From 1955 to 1959 he was associate editor of *John Bull*. Dudley Barker's books include biographies of Arnold Bennett and John Galsworthy, as well as a number of novels. As Lionel Black, Mr. Barker wrote a number of fast-moving stories of suspense, including *The Bait, Breakaway, Chance to Die, Outbreak, Swinging Murder,* and *Two Ladies in Verona.* Dudley Barker died in 1980.

DEATH HAS GREEN FINGERS

LIONEL BLACK

PENGUIN BOOKS

Penguin Books Ltd, Harmondsworth,
Middlesex, England
Penguin Books, 625 Madison Avenue,
New York, New York 10022, U.S.A.
Penguin Books Australia Ltd, Ringwood,
Victoria, Australia
Penguin Books Canada Limited, 2801 John Street,
Markham, Ontario, Canada L3R 1B4
Penguin Books (N.Z.) Ltd, 182–190 Wairau Road,
Auckland 10, New Zealand

First published in Great Britain by
the Collins Crime Club 1971
First published in the United States of America by
Penguin Books 1982

LIBRARY OF CONGRESS CATALOGING IN PUBLICATION DATA
Barker, Dudley.
Death has green fingers.
Reprint. Originally published: London:
Crime Club, 1971.
I. Title.
[PR6003.A679D4   1982]   823'.914   82-7537
ISBN 0 14 00.6282 3   AACR2

Printed in the United States of America by
George Banta Co., Inc., Harrisonburg, Virginia
Set in Baskerville

CHAPTER I

JONATHAN SIMS met them that Friday afternoon at Linchester station. 'You'll like Jonathan,' Henry had told his wife. 'Complicated sort of character, but amusing.' Kate Theobald had looked doubtful. Those of Henry's old college friends she had met so far had not seemed specially attractive; either dull or dissolute—most of them both. 'Not so sure about the girl he married,' Henry had gone on. 'South African, years younger than he is, father absolutely loaded with money, which is probably why Jonathan married her. He was never one, as they say, to let his heart rule his head. Though Stella's not bad-looking. Curvy brunette. Not as meticulous as some, I should guess, about her marriage vows.'

'She made a pass at you?'

'No, that was what was so irritating—at another man in the same party. Still, Jonathan didn't seem to mind too much. He was busy with a little blonde, one of his pupils at the university. I think it must be his specialty. Stella was one of his pupils before he married her.'

When he met them that Friday afternoon off the London train at Linchester station, Jonathan Sims was exactly what Kate had expected from her husband's vague description—tall, wide shoulders, narrow hips emphasized by tight-fitting jeans. His dark hair, cut to a length medium enough to arouse the contempt of neither senior nor junior common rooms, flowed thickly back from an interestingly sallow face; tall forehead, high cheekbones, brown eyes beneath dark brows, a thin nose, and lips full enough to suggest the sensual. Any female student of English language and literature at Wessex University whom Jonathan Sims wanted, Kate understood at once, would be a push-over. In the right mood, she could fancy him herself. Her hopes of the weekend brightened. She had expected it to be the combined boredoms of English village life and of the campus of the modern university down the road. Jonathan, it seemed, wanted a legal opinion on a business investment he had made for his mother which had gone dubiously wrong. And Henry Theobald, his old friend, was, after all, a barrister. 'So why don't you bring your wife to us for the weekend?' he had asked on the phone.

He had a languid, deep voice. 'Damn train is always twenty minutes late,' he complained as he led them from the station towards his elderly Austin car. 'But, since there's no conceivable reason for wanting to get here in a hurry, it doesn't much matter.'

For politeness, he put Kate in the seat next to his, but for most of the journey talked over his shoulder to Henry. Kate stared at the scenery. New places fascinated her. The car laboured its way up a steep hill into the main street of shops, which seemed just about all there was to Linchester, except for a couple of squares of brick Georgian houses with a view across the valley, and a set of grey stone buildings behind a tall brick wall.

'The county gaol?' she asked Jonathan.

'Yes. They say it's even more crowded than the university. That's the university, down there in the valley, beyond the trees. We pass it in a minute.'

The university buildings, mostly of glass, concrete and a hideous shade of red brick, and boldly sculpted in the modern manner, were scattered round what must have been good grazing land. 'Very impressive,' she murmured. Jonathan glanced sharply round at her, then slowly grinned.

Ashworth, the village, was a couple of miles farther. Kate saw at once that it was not a showplace. It straggled along the road—a village store that was also the post office, a few houses and bungalows, a row of cottages behind long gardens, a small grey church, vaguely Gothic, perhaps Early English; Kate's church architecture was more than shaky.

The Simses' house, in the middle of the village, was the Old Rectory; Victorian red brick, lushly garnished with rhododendrons, ancient yews and elms, impenetrable holly and laurel shrubberies. Stella Sims came quickly with the tea tray to the huge room at the back in which they evidently lived—book-lined, pleasantly shabby, littered with papers, sewing material, electronics and disc sleeves. Kate gazed covertly at the 'curvy brunette'. Henry had done her less than justice. The first impression was of large brown eyes, then of the gaiety of the smile, the beautifully-kept hands, the stare-worthy figure—and a plain fawn jersey suit which Kate priced enviously at a minimum of 60 guineas.

'Hope you don't mind being rushed out when you've scarcely set foot in the place,' Stella said. 'But we're bid to drinks with the local bachelor. We thought you might like to come.'

'Nick Bell,' added Jonathan. 'Quite a pleasant chap. Used to be some sort of businessman in the Far East, or South America, or some place. But he evidently made his pile early, and settled down here in the most charming small house in the district, and devoted himself to his two hobbies—roses and women.'

'In that order?' asked Kate, amused.

'Oh, I assure you. He's an amateur hybridist, and he's supposed to have had a success—a new floribunda, I think it is, with special qualities that, if it triumphs in the trials, will take it all over the world. Or so Nick says. I'm no rosarian myself. But he tells me it takes probably five years to produce a new rose, and another three or four before you know whether you've got a winner. Nick says,' he added, with that reflective grin of his, 'that he finds women much quicker.'

Sitting in the back of the car with Stella, Kate asked, 'Tell me something about the people we're likely to meet.'

'It's not a party—just a few people for drinks, Nick said. Usually that means a couple of couples from the university. He knows a lot of them, mainly through us. Then the local rose maniacs are usually there.'

'You have others?'

Stella laughed. 'My dear, this is a village of roses. It's because Cliffords' Nurseries are just up the road. You've heard of them? No? Well, they're not exactly Wheatcroft's or McGredy's. But they've been in the rose business for generations, man and boy. Jack Clifford runs it now. His father died a couple of years ago. Jack's a dear, and brilliant with roses, but they do say he's not such a good businessman, and he's been drinking a bit lately, perhaps because things are going wrong—I don't know. There's one story going round the village that there's domestic trouble.'

'Save us from village gossip,' interjected Jonathan from the front.

'Not half so bad as university gossip.'

He laughed. 'A university's only a village to the nth. What trouble's poor old Jack Clifford supposed to be having? Sally?'

'No, not Sally. Sally's Jack's wife,' she explained to Kate. 'Rather an odd sort of woman, difficult to know, very reserved, never opens up about anything. Her chief activity is horse-riding. She rides for hours pretty well every day. It's supposed to be Betty,' she told Jonathan.

'But she's only a child.'

'Fifteen or sixteen. Stories are, she's been running wild with the boys.'

8

'If that child goes wrong,' murmured Jonathan, 'it'll slay Sally—she's her life.'

'There may be nothing in it. I don't really know—probably mere gossip.'

'I adore gossip,' Kate assured her. 'After all, I work on a newspaper. It's our daily bread.'

'What fun it must be, that.'

Kate smiled ruefully. 'So they tell me. It's a job, like any other. But, to get back—the other rose maniacs.'

'The chief óne, besides Nick himself, is old Sir Gerald. Retired consul. The Argentine, I think, was his peak. He chatters like an old woman, drives a car like a lunatic—and he must be quite seventy—and has the most charming wife in the village. Rosa. Spanish originally, now all plump and cuddly, and white-haired and kind and delightful. She gives the impression of doing graceful good works all the time, but in fact does graceful nothing for anybody, being as lazy as hell—and everybody loves her for it. Now, who else?'

'Mamie Barrington,' supplied her husband, 'and Mrs Cordoni.'

Stella sighed. 'I suppose so. Nothing will keep Mamie from the smell of a cork. She's the local alcoholic, widow of a soldier, not in the least pathetic—she drinks fast and hard, and gets more intelligent and bitchier with every glass.'

'And Mrs Cordoni?'

'Nellie! She married an Italian, or says she did. If she did, he fled back to Italy years ago, like a sensible man. She's not bad-hearted, but she's the local grapevine. Knows everybody and everything. You can't go out to post a letter, but Nellie Cordoni knows—and probably knows to whom you're writing. Within minutes, it's all round the village. Of course, at least half of what she spreads is quite untrue. But she does it with such assurance . . .'

Jonathan had turned into a side lane, and soon drew up at Howth Lodge. It was indeed charming—black and white, thatch, old brick garden walls. Roses and clematis everywhere. The June sun had dropped sufficiently in the sky to show it up in a slanting light. Birds were singing like crazy.

'Old England indeed,' said Henry Theobald.

One car was already parked outside. As they emerged from theirs, they saw a man and woman standing in the porch.

'Sally and Jack Clifford,' introduced Stella. 'These are friends of Jon's, staying with us for the weekend, Kate and Henry Theobald. I've been telling Kate of the wonders of your nursery, Jack.'

'Are you interested in roses?'

'She's a newspaperwoman—she writes for the *Daily Post*,' said Stella. 'She's interested in everything.'

Kate felt again that the people they were meeting fitted their descriptions. Clifford was a fair-haired, rather plump man, going bald and a little grey at the temples, the skin of his face and the backs of his hands heavily sun-tanned, but the hands moving uneasily. The wife was just ordinary at first glance, but with more depth as you looked at her; certainly very shy and reserved, awkward and seemingly nervous simply to meet two strangers. She nodded, tried a brief smile, said nothing.

'Why don't we go in?' asked Jonathan.

'I've knocked a couple of times,' Clifford told him, 'and there's no answer.'

Jonathan tried the door handle. The door opened. He led the way into the main room—exposed beams, a huge inglenook filled with ferns, unimpressive furniture, a few undistinguished prints on the walls. Nick Bell didn't deserve such a charming house, Kate thought.

There were no signs of preparation for guests; no bottles out, no glasses.

'Have we got the day wrong?' asked Jack Clifford.
'No,' said Jonathan. 'I'm sure it was today.'

Through the front door came a tall, thin old man with
white moustache and straight back, followed by a plump
old woman with a thin black veil over her white hair, and
a dress that seemed to be floating with black veiling everywhere. 'The Hawkeses—Sir Gerald and his wife,' Stella
murmured to Kate.

Jonathan was explaining to the old man that there was
no sign of their host. They laughed and stood about
awkwardly. Others arrived. A Dr Wisbech and his wife,
from the Department of Natural Science at the university.
A fading, ageing blonde with the sharp eyes of a
terrier, who was evidently Mrs Cordoni. A retired Major
Somebody whose name Kate didn't quite catch, and his
thin daughter Mary. A gaunt-faced, intelligent-looking
woman on her own, Mamie Barrington, the local alcoholic with the bitter tongue. They stood around, trying
to chat, wondering what to do.

'I suppose Nick can't be working in his garden, and
have forgotten all about time,' suggested Sir Gerald,
smiling benignly.

Jonathan pushed open the french window. Some of
the others wandered after him. The garden, enclosed in
an old brick wall, consisted chiefly of several beds of
roses, each plant carefully labelled and code-numbered.
The white wooden door in the far wall stood open, disclosing a small paddock beyond, which also had been
cultivated as a rose ground.

'Have a look at Nick's roses, anyway,' invited Jonathan, leading Henry and Kate through the door. They
were nearly all in bloom, a delirious sight, even though
they were marshalled into squads and platoons, coded
and listed.

Kate turned back towards the gate at the same time
as the two men, and caught her breath simultaneously

with them. The door of the long, lean-to greenhouse against the outer side of the wall was open. Sprawled oddly against the bench lay a still figure. Although Henry tried to stop her, Kate pushed aside his arm and went forward with him; then blanched. In falling, the man's head had knocked several pots of roses on to the floor, and the blood that had flowed on to them had already congealed. The wound was in the side of the man's throat, from which still protruded the haft of a knife.

CHAPTER II

HENRY THEOBALD took charge; Jonathan seemed dazed. Henry put his arms round Kate's shoulders, swung her towards the gate. 'Back to the house. Come on, Jonathan. Who's your local policeman?'

Jonathan turned slowly, the sallowness of his face darkening. Kate thought he was going to vomit. But he suddenly recovered, hastening with them. 'Dick Vernon. Constable Vernon. He's got a house in the village. Hope to heavens he's home.'

'Suppose we ought to get a doctor,' said Henry, 'though it seems a bit pointless.'

'Duncan McKay. He lives in the village, but he's probably at his surgery in the town. I can't remember which nights he holds it.'

The people they had left were still standing awkwardly in the room. A few more, Kate saw, had arrived.

'Not there?' asked the tall, thin old ex-consul. She couldn't remember his name.

'Something dreadful's happened,' muttered Jonathan. Then he suddenly hurried across the room and took the arm of a newcomer, a stout man with a small grizzled moustache. 'Duncan. What luck you're here.' Jonathan turned to Henry. 'This is Dr McKay. Take him out there, will you, while I phone. Duncan, this is a friend of mine, Henry Theobald. Will you please go with him? It's very serious.'

'Of course,' said the doctor calmly. Kate noted approvingly he was not a man to be startled—a practical man. He followed Henry out into the garden.

'What on earth is it all about?' asked the ex-consul. Sir Gerald. Kate remembered his name now. Sir Gerald Hawkes. And the plump old dear was his wife, Rosa, whom everybody loved.

Jonathan said, 'Sit down, everybody, please. This is going to be a shock.' He paused. They all gradually settled. 'Nick is out there, in the greenhouse. He's dead.'

'Good heavens!' exclaimed Sir Gerald. 'A seizure?'

Jonathan shook his head. 'Murdered.'

In the moment of absolute silence, Kate instinctively glanced swiftly at the faces. Sir Gerald's jaw had dropped—it actually had, so the phrase was not meaningless. His wife looked merely puzzled, as though she had not really taken it in. Mamie Barrington, the alcoholic, was impassive, her dark lips pressed into a hard line. Jack Clifford, the rose nurseryman, had gone a nasty shade of dark red, as if something might burst. His wife's nervous expression had not changed, except that she had bitten on to her lower lip in horror. The soldier— Major Somebody whose name Kate had not caught —was staring hard at Mamie Barrington; an odd stare, almost apprehensive. His daughter Mary had her hand to her mouth in dismay. Stella Sims was gazing aghast at Jonathan. The college professor, Dr Wisbech, had gripped his wife's arm, as though to steady her. The only word to describe the expression on the face of Nellie Cordoni was 'agog'.

'Murdered?' cried Jack Clifford, in a throttled sort of voice. 'How do you mean, murdered?'

'Stabbed in the side of the throat with a pruning knife.'

'Good God!' from Sir Gerald.

Jonathan was making for the phone on the window ledge. 'Please be quiet. I'm going to phone Dick Vernon. We'll all have to wait, of course, until he gets here. Anybody know his number offhand?'

Clifford supplied it. Jonathan dialled. 'Hallo, is that Mrs Vernon? Jonathan Sims here. Is Dick in? Well, I'm sorry to interrupt him, but it's very important. Thanks.' He looked round while he waited, and murmured, with an odd laugh, 'Having his supper. Oh, hallo. Dick, you'll have to come round to Howth Lodge right away. Something awful's happened. Nick Bell has been killed. Yes, killed. Murdered.'

When he had put down the telephone, he turned again to the company with a nervous laugh. 'It'll take him five minutes to get here. What do we do? Polite conversation?'

'Tell us,' said Kate's anonymous soldier, 'exactly what happened when you went into the garden. Exactly what you saw.'

'I'll try,' said Jonathan. He began slowly, but there was so little to tell. They had stepped through the door in the wall, gazed at the roses for a few moments, then turned and seen the body in the greenhouse. He described how it appeared, the sprawl across the greenhouse staging, the pots of roses that had been knocked on to the floor and, in a lower voice, the haft of the knife, and the congealed blood. 'Horrible,' he muttered. Kate had a fear once again that he would be sick.

McKay and Henry came back. Everyone looked expectantly at the doctor.

'There's no doubt he's dead,' said McKay brusquely, 'so we didn't touch anything. Are the police informed?'

The rattle of a motorbike outside was his answer. The village constable came in; not the traditional peasant type, but a spruce young man, neat, precise. He would ask Mr Sims to show him exactly what had been found, and meanwhile would they all please remain where they were, and nobody leave the house? He went out with Jonathan, and was back almost at once, making for the telephone, reporting to his superiors.

Waiting for them to come, he took down statements from Jonathan, Henry and Kate on what they had seen—wrote them neatly and precisely in his notebook, and asked them to initial them 'as a matter of form, sir'. The fact that things were happening so meticulously, Kate noted, was already easing tension in the room. People were sitting back in their chairs, one or two getting out cigarettes, starting to talk to each other, though subdued. The only man, she thought, who was not relaxing was the soldier with the tremulous daughter. And now, when the constable spoke to him, she got his name. Major Sykes.

Once the police got there from Linchester, things moved fast. Cars pulled up outside, men went straight through the garden and the door in the wall. A middle-aged, somewhat stout, beery, jolly-looking policeman, obviously the highest in rank as yet, came into the cottage followed by a young, intellectual-faced assistant. University entrant, Kate guessed, and almost at once had her guess confirmed. The older man spoke to Constable Vernon, then nodded and went on into the garden, gesturing to his assistant to cope indoors. The younger man at once went up to Jonathan and addressed him by name.

'Damn glad it's you, Bill,' replied Jonathan. 'These two were with me when we found Nick—Mr and Mrs Theobald. They're our house-guests.' He laughed shortly.

'Damn queer weekend for guests. This is Detective Sergeant Bill Bates. He was at Wessex before he went into the police, so we all know him. Who's your boss?'

'Sam Kippis. Detective-Inspector. But he's only holding the fort until the Super gets here.'

'Wake himself?'

Bates nodded. 'He was out of town, but they reached him by radio. He's on his way.'

Kate asked: 'Is that Detective Chief Superintendent Roger Wake?'

'Yes. You're local, then?'

'No,' she told him. 'From London. But I work on a newspaper.'

The policeman looked alarmed. But Kate laughed and calmed him. 'Don't worry. After all, what have you said that I don't already know? But I need a phone pretty badly at the moment. Suppose I can use this one?'

Jonathan said: 'Better not. Use ours when we get home.'

'Hope it won't be long.'

It wasn't. The last police car drew up. From it came the tall, thin, slightly hunch-shouldered figure of Roger Wake. Kippis hurried out to meet him and they went on through the garden. Kate tried to remember what she could of Wake, from stories of previous cases he had handled. County force, of course; not the Yard. He'd been a bomber pilot in World War Two, won a rather good DFC, then entered the police on the beat. He was noted as a temperate man, drank almost nothing, non-smoker, rather reserved, disliked publicity although he knew that, grudgingly, he had to use it. One or two of his murder cases had been little classics of steady, patient routine police method, applied by a keen, deductive intelligence. 'Never takes a short cut,' one of the *Post*'s crime men had once told her, 'and never misses a hint.'

Kippis came back soon into the cottage. 'Ladies and gentlemen, there's no need to keep you any longer. The constable has a note of your names and addresses, but I don't think you'll be troubled much. Thank you for waiting so patiently.'

As they all stirred to leave, Kate went over to him. 'Inspector, I'm a reporter on the *Post*.'

He looked startled. 'Bit quick, that.'

Kate laughed. 'Pure coincidence, I'm afraid. But I'll have to phone a piece through, of course.'

'Can't stop you, miss.'

'But you can help. Has anything been found outside?'

'No more than was found by the two men and the girl who saw the body. You'd better ask them.'

Kate grinned. 'I'm the girl.'

Kippis responded with a rotund smile. He had a very jolly face, and a very beery nose. 'Then it's me who should be questioning you. No, absolutely nothing. We're policemen, not soothsayers.'

On the way back in the car she got what she could about Nicholas Bell from the Simses. But they knew little more than they had already told her. He had been in the village about 8 or 9 years, having retired from business somewhere abroad—Far East, Stella thought, but wasn't sure.

Had they any idea as to why he was murdered? 'I mean,' she said, 'had he a lot of enemies?'

'Could be,' said Jonathan curtly. 'He had a lot of women.'

After a pause, she asked if they had a picture of Bell.

Stella believed she could hunt out a couple of snapshots taken on a picnic the previous summer; not very good, but the newspaper might be able to make something of them.

'Are they your copyright? Who took them?'

'Jon did.'

'I'll see you get a fee,' she told Jonathan. He nodded absently. He was the one who had been most unstrung by the thing, although he was striving not to show it. It was probably a help to go on talking to him of trivialities such as snapshots and newspaper fees.

Back at the Old Rectory she made for the phone. When she had put her piece through, she switched to the night news desk.

'Nice piece, Kate,' said Butch. 'And very welcome. It's been a damn dull day.'

'Is it worth following up? Do you want me to stay on it? It may be dead by Monday.'

'You stay on it, Kate, and let us know if you want any help with the legwork. I've sent a photographer off to Linchester.'

'Horace?' she asked, and groaned when Butch said yes. Horace was a wonderful sneak photographer, but such a bore. 'I've got a couple of group snapshots that show Nicholas Bell. Not good, but I think you can blow him up enough. Henry is putting them on the train at Linchester. The eight-thirty-five. Will you collect them at the terminus?'

'Sure. Good girl. And if the story keeps running, concentrate on colour. Let's have more about those roses.' Butch chuckled. 'And one hell of a lot more about those women.'

CHAPTER III

'THE AWKWARD THING is that her newspaper has asked Kate to cover this murder,' Henry told Jonathan as they sat at breakfast in the kitchen. Both the wives had firmly chosen coffee and fruit in bed, which their respective husband had taken to them. Jonathan was frying bacon and eggs in a battered old pan, while Henry, under direction, set the kitchen table for the two of them and sliced bread for toast.

'What's awkward about that?'

'After all, we are your guests . . . Sure Stella won't mind? It seems a bit off, somehow.'

'Certainly she won't,' said Jonathan, coming across with the pan and shoving the food on to two plates. 'Nobody will think of anything else for a moment this weekend. To have a well-informed source actually in the house will be pure bliss for Stella. Coffee?'

Henry nodded. 'Of course, if it goes on longer than the weekend, we'll shift out into a pub.'

'Of course you'll do nothing of the kind. Just stay here. We shouldn't dream of letting you go.'

'Uncommon civil of you,' murmured Henry, embarrassed.

When he got back to the bedroom, Kate was coming from her bath, wrapped in a bath-sheet. 'Forgot my dressing-gown. I'll buy one in Linchester this morning. And keep your filthy hands to yourself, if *you* please, Mr Theobald. I have work to do.'

'On Saturday? But there's no *Post* on a Sunday. You don't have to send another piece until tomorrow evening.'

'But to-day'll be the day, darling,' she told him, pulling on her clothes. 'All the crime boys turned up last night. They say the Nag's Head hasn't had a night like it since VE Day. Now it'll go to the usual pattern. Today, being the first day, they'll all interview the police. From then on, all the reporters will be in the bar, interviewing each other. They get more interesting stories that way. How about the Simses?'

'Jonathan was very co-operative. He swears Stella

will be intrigued to have the horse's mouth, as it were, in the privacy of her home. And he won't hear of us leaving if it goes on after tomorrow.'

'That's as well. Horace—our photographer—yes, I know, dreadful isn't it?—got the last attic at the Nag's Head last night, sharing with two legmen from the *Express* and a wire man from the *Mirror*.'

'All the same, it's a bit embarrassing.'

'Doesn't embarrass me. What is troubling me is that I've only one pair of ears. And I'll have to waste a good part of the day at the police station. There's bound to be a press conference. Do you want to help?'

'Why not? If one of us is going to rat on our hosts, we may as well both. What can I do?'

'Butch wants all the colour he can get about the women, and the roses—Nick Bell's two hobbies, remember? I'll do the work on the women. Will you take on the roses?'

'Sure. What do you want to know?'

'Just what Bell was doing. What does a hybridist do? I'm damn vague about it—and so, I'll bet, are most of our readers, in spite of the Gardening Page. Documentary background, darling, that's what I want. Why not go and see the ex-consul? He's a rose maniac, and Stella said he chatters like an old woman. Take a taxi on expenses if it's far, but I think it's only just down the next lane. I've rented a self-drive car, by the way, and named us both as drivers. It'll be here soon.'

'And how do you intend to start work on the women?'

'Nellie Cordoni. I don't suppose it'll be difficult. All I'll have to do is go to her house and put a few direct questions. But if I don't get there soon, she'll start telling it to the first person in the street, or bust.'

When she reached the house, Kate almost laughed aloud at her accuracy. Mrs Cordoni, scarf round head and shopping basket over arm for camouflage, was just emerging from her front door.

'I'm Kate Theobald, staying with the Simses.'

'Of course. What a frightful thing it was, us all standing there, not knowing that poor Nicky was out in the greenhouse . . . I'm still shaking with shock. Of course, you're the newspaper reporter. My dear, if I can help . . . Come in.'

The main room of the cottage was L-shaped, with a french window leading out into a small, well-tended garden. A large grey cat was asleep in the sun on the stone path outside the window. The room was as crammed with objects as Mrs Cordoni with gossip. One or two pieces of furniture were worth money, probably heirlooms from Nellie's family; especially a charming small bureau, and a folding mahogany card-table against the wall next to the hearth. Photographs, ornaments and souvenirs everywhere. A pair of hideous blue vases picked out in gilt, standing on a shelf with two or three figures that were probably Chelsea of a decent period. A scatter of cushions, a half-finished cotton frock, a whorl of grey knitting, magnificent roses arranged quite well in a green-and-gilt bowl, a selection of fans in the fireplace, dried bulrushes in a tall vase, a worn leather address-book by the telephone.

'What I want to know,' started Kate, accepting the gestured armchair, 'is as much as possible about Mr Bell—the people he knew, the things he did.'

Nellie Cordoni folded her hands on her lap and raised her eyes in supplication to the ceiling. 'Where to start, my dear! He was a very charming man, mind you. And *de mortuis*, etc. But you need facts for your newspaper.'

Kate inclined her head encouragingly. 'He had some girl-friends, I hear.'

The eyes went up again. 'My dear, notorious! There's no other word for it. And if the police don't know where to look, there are one or two of us as could tell them.'

'Where to look?'

Nellie Cordoni regarded her appraisingly, as though trying to judge how much she would understand. 'Let me put it this way. The girl-friends were not just silly young girls, if you follow me.'

'Women. Married women?'

She nodded emphatically. 'There are some things I've seen with my own eyes . . .' She motioned Kate to the window and pointed down the lane. 'You see that white gate?'

At once Kate recognized it. 'That's Howth Lodge? I'd no idea you were so close.' She smiled. 'You certainly have a vantage point, Mrs Cordoni.'

'I can't help seeing. I happen to look out of my window, and there . . . Well!'

'So it's your idea that Nick Bell was killed by a jealous husband?'

Mrs Cordoni primmed her lips. 'I'm not saying what's my idea, and what isn't. But can you see this as anything but a crime of passion?'

'It is,' Kate admitted, 'a quite frequent motive.'

'Well, I'd better say no more.'

'Would any of the women be among those at Howth Lodge last night?'

'Oh, dear me. If you put that sort of thing in your newspaper, I shall find myself sued for libel.'

'Don't worry,' Kate assured her. 'We're much too careful. And we never disclose our sources of information.'

Mrs Cordoni gazed at her speculatively for a long moment. Then she asked, 'Are the Simses great friends of yours?'

'Jonathan was at Oxford with my husband. I'd never met either of them until yesterday.'

Mrs Cordoni expired with relief. 'Then I can speak a little more freely.'

'Do you mean,' asked Kate, 'that Stella Sims was having an affair with Nick Bell?'

'I'm not saying what I mean, or what I don't mean. She's a dear, sweet girl, and who could blame her, the way Jonathan carries on with that child at the university. Have you met Anne Brodie? Believe me, my dear, if you stay long with the Simses, you will. She's always there.'

'One of his pupils?'

'I see you know more than you admit.'

'Oh, I just heard a chance remark,' said Kate. She was trying to assess what truth there might be in the woman's hints. But Henry, on his previous visit, had noticed something of the kind.

'You could say,' Nellie Cordoni went on, 'that pretty well all the women you met last night . . .'

'Except you, I take it.'

'You're right. Although if Nicky Bell had had his way . . . But I won't go into that. Except me, and except Lady Hawkes.'

'Well now,' recollected Kate calmly, 'just who was there? Mrs Clifford?'

'No, I wouldn't necessarily say Sally Clifford. Poor old Jack has his problems, but over Betty, their daughter. Only fifteen, and already in trouble with the boys.'

'In trouble?'

'That I wouldn't know. But she's certainly been carrying on with a few of the boys—and I wouldn't be hard put to name a couple. Now she's gone away to stay with Jack's cousin in London, and I shouldn't be in the least bit surprised if we didn't see young Betty again for nine months. Not that I know anything, mind you.'

Kate was coming to the opinion that this was about right—Nellie Cordoni didn't know anything. Or rather, she knew a few things, and gossiped wildly about everything else. That made her even less reliable. She herself probably didn't know with exactitude what was true, what was half-true, what was guessing, and what invention. Still, it was worth letting her talk. The chatter might include a hint that could be fruitful.

'You said pretty well all the women I met last night. Mrs Barrington? Oh, but that won't do. She's a widow, isn't she? So there can't be any jealous husband.'

'She never married again,' agreed Nellie Cordoni, with a meaning glance, 'in the sight of the Church.'

'But is there someone?'

'There is a *friend*. More than that I cannot say.'

'And the friend is . . .?'

'Wilfred Sykes, who else? You met him last night with his daughter Mary. Major Sykes.'

'Another soldier. Mrs Barrington's husband was a soldier, wasn't he?'

Nellie nodded. 'Colonel Barrington. He was killed in action in the campaign against the Communists in Malaya. Nobody here knew him, of course, but Mamie once told me the boy is the spit of his father. Ralph—that's her son—is rising sixteen now. He was born out in Malaya, not long before his father was killed.'

'The boy lives in the village?'

'Yes, but he's at his boarding school. You've probably heard how much Mamie drinks. Quite terrifying, my dear, I assure you. But when Ralph is home for the holidays, she never touches it.'

The woman's face came back into Kate's recollection; hard, sombre and, she now suddenly understood, agonized. Kate no longer wanted to discuss Mamie Barrington with this village gossip. To turn the subject, she brought up another of last night's women, the university professor's wife.

'Laura Wisbech?' Nellie Cordoni took up. 'Now, there's an interesting person.'

'She's certainly a very pretty woman. But I thought she looked ill.'

'You newspaper reporters don't miss anything.'

'You mean she is ill?'

'Some might call it illness. I call it self-indulgence. But I suppose, in this permissive age . . .'

Kate got it at once. 'You mean drugs?'

'Never mind what I mean, my dear. Next time you meet Laura Wisbech, take a look at her eyes and form your own opinion.'

'And the supply? Are you hinting the supplier was Nick Bell?'

'Oh, that,' replied Nellie Cordoni, refolding her hands with dignity in her lap, 'I really couldn't say.'

Kate laughed, rose from her seat and wandered towards the window. 'Your village seems to be quite something with the lid off.'

Was any of it true? she wondered. Or was it all the revenge fantasies of a woman whose husband had left her; or was the husband too a fantasy, dreamed up by a yearning old maid? It was becoming clearer to Kate that she was wasting her time. Looking along the lane, she idly asked, 'Were you at home yesterday, Mrs Cordoni? If so, you must have seen anybody who went to Howth Lodge.'

Mrs Cordoni did not stir in her seat. Kate looked round, surprised at the silence. 'Well, did you?'

The other nodded. 'Mr Tooth went in during the morning, about midday I reckon it was, with a crate of bottles.'

'Bottles? A wine merchant? No, of course, the chap

who keeps the village pub, the Nag's Head. I suppose he was delivering the drink we were to have in the evening.'

'I suppose so,' conceded Nellie Cordoni. 'They do say in the village that Nick Bell got his drinks from Billy Tooth for nothing. Billy owed him so much money. Of course, that was only rumoured. But Billy did lose a lot of money on the horses, that I do know. He's a gambler, Mrs Theobald, and can't leave the horses alone.'

'Still, there's nothing very suspicious in a publican delivering bottles. Who else?'

'Sir Gerald drove up about an hour after Billy Tooth had left. He came in that car of his, much too fast, as always, and his brakes squealed when he stopped. It was what brought me to the window. I thought there might have been an accident. But when I saw the car, I knew it was only Sir Gerald, the way he always drives. An old man like that, too! But he didn't stay more than a few minutes. Got out of his car, went into the Lodge, and soon came out again, got into his car and rushed off, usual fashion.'

'Why do you think he stayed such a short time?'

'Probably just looked in to say he and Rosa would be there in the evening, or leave a little note if he didn't find Nick about.'

Could be, thought Kate. But the reason for the short visit didn't matter. By its very shortness, it clearly didn't involve murder.

'Anybody else?'

'How can I tell? I don't spend my time sitting at this window, watching who goes to call at Howth Lodge. Earlier that morning, for instance, I didn't see Mamie Barrington go there.'

Puzzled, Kate asked, 'You mean, she didn't go there?'

'Oh, she went there all right. I happened to see her

come out. I just went to do a bit of weeding in my windowbox, so I couldn't help seeing her. But plenty of people could have come and gone without my knowing. Don't imagine, young woman, that I sit here spying on people, or I shall get offended, I assure you.'

Kate put the question bluntly. 'Who else was there that you're trying not to tell me about?'

Nellie hesitated, stroked her fingers doubtfully, looking down at them. 'I'm not sure I should say anything about it. There was another man went in, about half past two. I'd finished my lunch, and I happened to be sitting here in the window, drinking a cup of coffee. The sun was out, and it was very nice and warm in the window—'

'Who was he?'

'Mr Sims.'

'Jonathan?' cried Kate, astonished, then suddenly, for no particular reason, afraid. Afraid of what, or for whom? she demanded of herself. Afraid, she knew, for Stella. Even in so short a time she had come to like Stella Sims. Could she really have been having it off with the man who had been killed? Could it possibly be Jonathan Sims who . . .? She gathered herself quickly. 'I suppose he had some message to deliver.'

'He was there quite a long time. In fact, I was just going down to try to catch him—I wanted to settle a couple of points about the flower show this afternoon; he promised to lend a hand with the sideshows. So I went to get my hat, and I had just left the house and was walking down the lane when he came out of the Lodge, rather quickly, and got into his car. I don't think he saw me. I called out, "Mr Sims". But he didn't seem to hear me. He just started up the car and drove away.'

'So then you came back here?'

'Of course, my dear. I'd missed him.' She paused, looking down again at her hands, then straight at

27

Kate. 'I've been wondering. Do you think I ought to tell Police Constable Vernon?'

'No reason why not,' answered Kate as carelessly as she could. 'But I don't suppose he'll be very interested. Jonathan is bound to have told the police about his visit, you can be sure of that.'

'Ah yes, of course he will have,' breathed Nellie contentedly.

Kate rose to go. She was feeling a little sick in her stomach.

There was no ducking the press conference. She had to be there.

The street outside Linchester police station was jammed with vehicles. But when she showed her press pass, a constable waved her into the police park behind the building.

They were all there, of course; the evenings and Sundays boys in strength, and at least one from each of the dailies. Several of the photographers were cursing the BBC driver who had backed across their path for a vantage point for his own cameraman on the roof of his van. The other television news outfit was grouped closely round the door into the station.

Kate waved, and greeted a few of her friends; then wished she had not, for it attracted the attention of Horace, her own photographer, who broke off a loud argument with a couple of policemen to cross over to her. Wherever he went, Horace caused trouble. He wore a sense of personal grievance like a badge of office. It was said he once went into Claridge's bar at the most reverend cocktail hour and demanded raucously to be told whether it was a Watney house. He always bought a second-class rail ticket, charged first-class on his expenses sheet—and always, of course, travelled in a first-class carriage, usually complaining bitterly about his fellow passengers. Once, when a woman got in with a full-size French poodle on a lead, he summoned the guard, enquired loudly whether British Railways expected their first-class passengers to travel in the company of a lion, and had the dog locked in the guard's van. When the woman angrily lit a cigarette, he pointed out to her, with emphatic politeness, that she was in a non-smoker.

'Look here, Kate,' he chided her, 'I'm not getting much co-operation. You haven't given me a clue about what pictures to get.'

'Do your own homework, Horace.'

'Come on, now. That's not quite the attitude from a colleague.'

'Just take your little snapshots of them all,' she advised sweetly, 'and try not to muddle the captions.'

His retort was cut by seeing Inspector Kippis emerge from the station to give the television men a camera interview (in which, of course, he would reveal nothing except calm confidence). Horace rushed off to mix in the crowd of jostling lenses.

The small back office of the station was already too full, and thick with the usual institutional sanitary smell. With everybody talking, the chatter was deafening. The only perch she could find was an uncomfortably corrugated, cold radiator. She thanked her stars she was not often put on crime stories. Unsatisfactory disclosures by suspicious policemen, drinking in pubs with detectives, rushing round late at night on a rumour that some rival had turned up a new witness—not her idea of a quiet newspaper life. She sighed, and grimaced at a man from one of the Sundays, Dereck Andrews, an old friend, who spent all his spare time working at a long, immensely learned study of Beckett (the playwright, not the martyr), and reported criminal offences for a living. He grimaced cheerfully back, being too far off to talk to her.

Roger Wake came in quickly through a back door and took the centre of the three chairs behind the desk. Kippis, the beery-cheery detective, sat on his right, and a policeman Kate had not previously seen on his left. She looked with curiosity at Wake himself. She had heard that he rarely took press conferences, preferring to leave them to a subordinate. But she supposed he felt he had to appear at the first one. He was obviously uneasy, disliking the necessity. He had already picked up a pencil on the desk and was playing with it nervously. A couple of times he pushed his fingers through his untidy, slightly curly brown hair. His hands were uncommonly long, thin and bony. His grey eyes were by no means penetrating or keen; their expression somewhat vague, almost dreamy. But he did not lower his gaze to the desk. He looked slowly, unfalteringly round the room, then began: 'Good morning, ladies and gentlemen . . .' His voice was difficult to place—neither cultivated nor rough, and much deeper than Kate had expected. He was making the usual request for their co-operation, and assuring them that all facts that could safely be released would be communicated to them at once. Detective-Inspector Kippis, whom he thought most of them knew, would act as their contact with the police. And now he would ask Mr Kippis to give them such information as was already available.

Sam Kippis smiled amiably and began: 'There's damn little. A retired businessman named Nicholas Bell, who lived alone at Howth Lodge in the village of Ashworth, was found murdered yesterday evening by three of the guests he had invited to a cocktail party at his house. He was in the greenhouse in his garden, and had been stabbed in the side of the throat with some sort of gardening knife, which was probably his own—there were several like it in the greenhouse. He appeared to have been struck twice, for in addition to the wound that killed him there was another shallow gash on the front of his throat.

'He was found, as you probably already know, by Mr Jonathan Sims, a lecturer at Wessex University, who also lives in Ashworth, and two friends staying with him for the weekend, Mr and Mrs Henry Theobald, who have some sort of connection with the press.'

He grinned. All eyes swivelled to Kate. 'Henry's not talking,' she told them blandly, 'except to the *Post*. He's tied up.'

Amid the laughter, Kippis resumed: 'There's not much else to tell you yet. It's obviously murder. I think you can say foul play is suspected! But we don't yet have any idea as to the identity of the murderer, or the motive, except that it doesn't appear to have been theft. Mr Bell was known locally to be in the habit of keeping fairly large sums of money in the house. In fact, there was just over three hundred pounds in notes in a cashbox in a cupboard in the dining-room, but there was no sign that anybody had been trying to find it. The cupboard door was locked, with quite a good lock, and no attempt had been made to force it. Otherwise, up to now your guess is as good as ours —and probably a damn sight more imaginative.'

They were laughing again, and the questions were shooting at Kippis. 'What do you know about Bell?' 'Any fingerprints on anything, Sam?' 'How long had he beed dead?'

'We haven't had a full report yet from the forensic-medicine chaps. But that side of it is a bit difficult. Bell was certainly killed yesterday, but the timing is uncertain. The body was in a greenhouse, which had heated up a good deal with the sun, although the door was open. No, the heating system wasn't being used. I suppose he turned that on only in the winter. But the body being under glass makes it tricky to calculate timing.

It's being worked on. There were fingerprints, of course, all over the cottage, and some in the greenhouse. But so far the only ones we've found in the greenhouse were Mr Bell's own. And his own prints were the only ones on the knife—which doesn't mean we think he stabbed himself in the throat!'

'What does it mean?'

'Ask me that question a bit later, Bill. It could mean the killer wore gloves—that's the most likely. But there are other possibilities which will, I don't doubt, occur to you.'

'What do you know about Bell?'

'Not much as yet,' Kippis cheerfully admitted. 'He had lived there about eight years. He was an amateur rose-grower. According to one newspaper report this morning, he had a lot of girl-friends.'

The eyes came round to Kate again.

'Is it true?' one of the *News of the World* men asked Kippis.

'Don't be rude, Fred,' said Kate.

Kippis smiled. 'I always believe what I read in the newspapers, Fred. And I feel fairly sure it'll be in the *News of the World* tomorrow. So it must be true, eh?'

An older man, near the front, who had been taking a careful shorthand note and must therefore be the reporter from the local newspaper, put a question to Wake himself: 'Will you be calling in Scotland Yard, Mr Wake?'

For the first time, Roger Wake smiled. 'Not at this stage, anyhow, Mr Gilbert. Of course, if I get completely baffled . . .'

The questions went on and on. None elicited much. The truth, Kate felt sure, was that the police simply didn't know any more yet. When they did, the 'no comment' answers would begin. But for the present

Kippis was answering with apparent candour and great good humour.

There was one question that Kate herself wanted to ask, but hesitated to put. Then suddenly it came from a man to her left. 'Do you know of anybody who was at Howth Lodge yesterday?—before the drinks party in the evening, I mean.'

'The landlord from the Nag's Head, Mr Billy Tooth, went there to deliver a case of spirits at about noon,' replied Kippis. 'He didn't see Bell, and there was nobody else in the house or in the garden. But this was quite usual. He did as he often did—opened the door and left the delivery in the kitchen. Otherwise, we know of nobody who was there yesterday before Mr and Mrs Clifford, from the rose nursery, were the first of the invited guests to arrive in the evening.'

Kate heard him with a snatch of dread. Jonathan Sims had spent half an hour with the police the previous evening, giving them all the information he could about Nick Bell, and exactly what had happened when he and the Theobalds found the body.

Why hadn't he told them of his own visit to Howth Lodge at half past two in the afternoon?

CHAPTER IV

INTRODUCING HIMSELF on the telephone, Henry Theobald said to Sir Gerald: 'I wonder if you would help us, sir. My wife is reporting this awful business for her newspaper, since we happened to be the ones who first saw Mr Bell's body.'

'Ah, you are the pleasant young couple staying with the Simses.'

'That's right. At least, I hope we're pleasant. Our name is Theobald, Kate and Henry. My wife writes for the *Post*. I'm at the Bar.'

'Very interesting. In what way can I help you?'

'Kate wants some information about hybridizing roses. Background material, you know. Bell was an amateur rosarian, it seems.'

'Indeed he was—and most successful. I've always maintained that there's no such thing as having green fingers. You either do the job properly and get results, or you don't, and fail. But when I think of the luck Nicky Bell had with his roses—well, I begin to believe in green fingers after all. But there, of course I should be delighted to tell your wife whatever I can about roses.'

'She's rather tied up with all the police business, sir. I was wondering whether, if I myself came along, you would be kind enough . . .'

'Yes, of course. Come now, if you like.'

'Thanks, I will. Jason's Farmhouse, isn't it? In Pinchback Lane. I'm told I can walk it in ten minutes.'

It was an old grey stone farmhouse. The garden in front was quite small, very neat, but not specially well planted except for a circular bed of deep red roses. The wistaria that covered the front wall of the house had ceased blooming weeks earlier. But there was a spiky cluster of lupins and delphiniums against an old stone wall, topped by a purple clematis in rich bloom, that seemed almost ludicrously to be posed for a watercolour drawing, 'In the Garden'.

Sir Gerald, in a pair of canvas slacks, a pale blue shirt open at the neck, and an old straw hat, came round the side of the house to greet him. 'Rosa insists that we take coffee with her. It's much too hot for coffee, but, like a wise man, I always do what my wife tells me. Ah, but you're married too, eh?' He gave a

34

little, high-pitched chuckle and led the way into the house.

The room was done out delightfully in pale green and white. The furniture was old, large, comfortable, clothed in faded chintz covers. The walls, shelves, piano top, occasional tables, were smothered with ancient photographs of people in tropical clothes posing placidly under palm trees, ornaments and curios from Mediterranean or South American countries, photographs of a young man in naval uniform who was obviously their son, and of a girl in the white gown and feathered headdress in which long ago she had been presented to Her Majesty. Among all these were littered stacks of books in faded bindings, gardening catalogues, a television receiver that could not have been less than ten years old, and Lady Hawkes herself, seated at her coffee-table in a flowered dress that made no attempt to hide her comforting rotundity. She welcomed Henry: 'This dreadful thing about poor Nicky Bell, Mr Theobald!' Her voice still had a faintly foreign flavour, an attractive lingering on consonants, a musical roundness of vowels. 'Will you take cream or milk in your coffee? And sugar?'

He took cream and no sugar. He chatted amiably with them about the cleverness of his wife being a newspaper writer, the heat of this particular summer, the regrettable rise in the price of quite basic commodities such as whisky, and the exciting new orchids at the Chelsea Show. The Hawkeses were delightful—professionally so. Thus, in various sultry climates, had they spread the legend of the equanimity and charm of the British. Had they ever in their lives, Henry wondered, suffered any real distress? Had either of them ever done a day's hard work? As a consul, Sir Gerald would probably not have had to fight in either of the world wars (though

Henry had no doubts of his patriotism or, if required, courage; but probably it never had been required). As the consul's wife, Lady Hawkes had never been without efficient servants, may never have had to cook a meal, until his retirement. And now, although they suffered the hardship of returning to a land of indifferent climate and no servants, they were still clothed with professional amiability and self-satisfaction as though with a warm suit of armour. Nor was the hardship so severe—a pleasant house in a small village, all the money they needed, interesting news now and then from the children who were too old and too distant to cause any bother; a life for her requiring not much energy, and, for him, the obsession of the roses.

He was already talking of the roses. 'But if I start I shall go on for ever. Tell me exactly what you want to know.'

'Well,' began Henry, 'I take it that a hybridist is somebody who tries to produce a new rose by artificially crossing one species with another.'

'Not species. You cross one hybrid with another hybrid. Look here, the elements of the thing are quite simple. The species are the natural roses of the world —the wild roses, if you like. The ones the Almighty created.' He laughed pleasantly. 'You must forgive a gardener his reverence for Nature. There are known to be something more than a hundred species of natural roses, and some of them have been living on this planet longer than *Homo sapiens*!'

'How do we know?'

'Recognizable fossils.'

'Fascinating,' said Henry.

Lady Hawkes smiled kindly at him and got up slowly from her chair. 'I have heard the lecture before, Mr Theobald. I know you will excuse me.'

When she had gone, Sir Gerald laughed again, his

high-pitched, cultivated, elderly little laugh. 'I bore everyone, I'm afraid. But I'll shorten the lecture as much as I can. The French Rose and the China Rose are the two main ancestors of the modern hybrid Tea roses. I won't trouble you with their botanical names. The China Rose came from China, where so many of the rose species are found. The French Rose didn't originate in France, but is said to have been brought to that country by a returning Crusader. And, ever since, France has been one of the great rose-breeding countries of the world. It's only for the last hundred years or so that England, other European countries, and the United States have taken up rose-breeding importantly.

'Well now, Mr Theobald, those two rose species were the ancestors of the Damask roses, the Bourbon roses, the Cabbage roses and, among others, the Tea roses—the Tea roses, which came to Europe from China in the last century, were so called because their fragrance reminded people of the smell of the chests in which tea was imported from the East. Then two other strains of roses were added to the family tree, one species called the Persian Yellow, and one called *Rosa multiflora* which is especially valuable for its qualities of free flowering and strong growth. In very general terms, this is how we have produced the modern floribunda roses. And what we rosarians work on now is crossing hybrid Teas or hybrid floribundas, in an attempt to produce a new rose of some special colour or quality. The most popular goal nowadays is to try to get a truly blue rose. A lot of people have got near it, but all the roses have had a touch of lavender colouring—not blue in the sense that a delphinium or a forget-me-not is blue.' He laughed again. 'It easily becomes a life-long obsession which drives you pleasantly mad.'

In this country drawing-room on a warm summer's day, Henry found it delightfully indolent to listen to an old man talking with such enthusiasm of roses. 'How's it done, Sir Gerald?' he lazily asked.

'Come and see,' Sir Gerald happily invited him, leading the way through the french window into the garden behind the house. 'I play about with the thing myself.'

'I'm putting you to a great deal of trouble, sir.'

'Nothing gives me greater pleasure than to show off my little rose establishment, I assure you. Everybody round here is either engrossed in his own roses, or runs away with a piercing scream at the very sound of the word.'

The garden was enclosed in a mellow stone wall at least eight feet in height, from which the warmth of the sun gently glowed. It was not a large garden, almost entirely taken up by beds of roses separated by narrow grass verges; the roses all carefully labelled, many of them covered with blooms, the best of which were protected by paper cones like fools' caps, fixed on canes.

One of the four walls was occupied by a lean-to greenhouse, its panes shaded with green blinds. It was here that Sir Gerald led Henry, gesturing to the rose plants ranged in pots on the staging.

'Now, Mr Theobald, you see this rose here. This is Red Dandy, a floribunda rose of the hybrid Tea type and, as you see, bright scarlet crimson in colour. I propose, let us say, to use this as the male plant in the marriage I am arranging—on the whole, the colour of the male is more likely to be transmitted to the offspring. From the female they tend to get strength and growth.

'So for the female I choose, say, Meilland's most famous rose, Peace, which is very vigorous. See this fully-formed bud of the Peace, not yet fully opened? I carefully pull off all the petals. Now you see the female pistils in the centre, with the male stamens around them.

The stamens have at their tip the anthers which produce the pollen. The pistils are tipped with stigmas which become sticky and hold the pollen, which eventually fertilizes the rose and produces seeds.'

As he was talking, the old man was removing the petals of the rose with astonishing deftness. Then, picking up a small, razor-sharp knife from the bench, he began to cut off all the stamens, putting them carefully aside. 'They will be destroyed. We don't want to fertilize our Peace rose with its own pollen, but with pollen from Red Dandy.'

He picked up a small piece of white paper, twisted it into a neat cone and placed it gently over the rose. 'That will prevent any chance pollination as the stigmas ripen. They'll take a couple of days or so. When they are ripe, I shall use this little camel-hair brush to pick up pollen from one of the Red Dandy blooms—you can see it here, collecting inside the petals where it has fallen. I shall brush it on to the stigmas of the Peace, which will by then be sticky. Then back goes the paper cone, and I wait for anything up to a week to tell if fertilization has taken place.'

'How do you tell?'

'The seed pod here begins to swell. By autumn it will be a ripening hep. I shall bury the hep in the garden, stuck around with holly leaves to keep off mice. By Christmas it will have rotted, and I can pick out the seeds. I throw away any that float on water; they're not fertile. Those that sink under water I plant in sterilized compost next January. By late spring I shall have some seedlings to transplant into boxes or pots. By this time next year will come the first flowers on the seedlings, and I can start to tell if any of my crosses have produced a worthwhile rose.'

Henry asked: 'What are the chances?'

With his high-pitched chuckle, Sir Gerald replied:

'Dishearteningly small. I don't know if you have ever studied your Mendel? No? Well, genetically, the chances of combining two known characteristics—one from the male and one from the female—in a new rose are at least 64 to one against. In practice, because there are so many different characteristics in each of the hybrids you are using, the chances of getting a new rose worth going on with are at least 100,000 to one against. I've heard it put pessimistically at a million to one. A keen amateur I know made 2,500 cross-pollinations one year, using 355 different sets of parents. He gathered something like 50,000 seeds, all carefully indexed and catalogued according to their parents. He succeeded in raising about 24,000 seedlings. Then you have to bud these on to seedling stock—most roses grow better, as you probably know, not on their own roots, but on the roots of wild roses, usually dog-roses, briars. My friend budded about 800 seedlings. Fewer than 100 of those were worth going on with a year later. The following year he reduced the number to eleven. In the end he got five roses which were good enough to pass over to a nurseryman to propagate. But none was a real winner—after six years of patient, demanding work. What a hobby, eh, Mr Theobald? My goodness, we must all be mad.'

'Have you had any outstanding successes, Sir Gerald?'

'Not outstanding, although three of my roses have been thought good enough to send to the trial grounds of the Royal National Rose Society—with what results I shall not know until next year. I dare not hope for a medal, but am fairly confident of a Trial Ground Certificate. That is the extent of my success so far.' He paused, looked hard at Henry, gave another little high-pitched chuckle and demanded, 'Can you keep a great secret, Mr Theobald?'

'You have my word.'

Sir Gerald led the way out of the greenhouse and

made towards the far end of the garden. About half-a-dozen rose bushes were sunk in their pots in a separate small bed, each protected by paper cones. The ex-consul carefully removed one of the cones and stepped back, his eyes shining. The bloom was blue. Not a deep blue. More like a light Cambridge blue. But blue.

'Would you say there's still a touch of pink in it?' he anxiously asked.

Henry shook his head. 'I'm no expert, but it looks blue to me.'

Reverently the old man replaced the paper cone. 'I think I have won,' he mused, 'although now the victory is hollow. Poor Nicky Bell and I were having a friendly race. He claimed that he and Dr Wisbech had a blue rose for the first time this summer. He and Wisbech worked together, you know. Wisbech is a most talented botanist. I can't tell. He invited nobody to see his rose, not even me.' He cackled again. 'On the other hand, I never invited him to see mine, Mr Theobald. Indeed, I never let on to him, or anybody else, that I had a blue rose. I am telling you now because in a few days' time a friend of mine, an expert official of the Rose Society, is coming to inspect my rose. Then there can be no further question about it. I beg you to say nothing to anybody until then, Mr Theobald. Perhaps I shouldn't have shown you my rose, but I was carried away—your sympathetic interest, my dear young man, and my own enthusiasm. Give me your word again, I beg you.'

'Of course, Sir Gerald.'

'After all, Nicky Bell talked too much, and too soon.'

Henry stared at him in surprise. 'Surely you are not suggesting . . . But that's absurd. Who would commit murder for a rose?'

The old man chuckled nervously. 'Obsessions can go to astonishing lengths. Let me hasten to assure you

41

that mine has not done so. After all,' he said with a smile, 'I have my own blue rose.'

'I can't believe it. Murder for a rose? All that risk for the sake of a flower?'

'And its value, Mr Theobald. Don't forget its value.'

'Has a new rose any value, then? Commercially, you mean?'

'Certainly. You can now get protection under the law, so that you profit by your patience and your work—if you are very, very lucky.'

Putting on his calm law-court manner, Henry asked: 'Are you suggesting that somebody might have killed Bell in order to steal his rose?'

'It is surely a possibility. Do you know, Mr Theobald, how much a really successful new rose might be worth?'

'No, I confess I don't.'

'Since old Meilland produced Peace in 1942,' said Sir Gerald slowly, 'I suppose it must have made something in the neighbourhood of £100,000. I'm only guessing. But it must probably be something of that order.'

Henry stared at him in astonishment. He had turned his own gaze back to the plant he had just shown Henry.

'One breeds roses for the joy of it, and the glory of producing a new variety,' he said softly. 'But how much do you think a genuinely blue rose, that kept its characteristics through the trials, might be worth?'

CHAPTER V

THERE WAS NO OPPORTUNITY for Kate to talk to Henry before lunch. By the time she got back from Linchester to the Old Rectory, he was already having a gin and tonic with the Simses on the terrace at the back of the house. And, as Nellie Cordoni had correctly foretold, Jonathan's girl friend from the university was with them. 'One of my students, Anne Brodie,' Jonathan introduced her. She was pretty enough, blonde, rather small. Kate had the impression that she was tense about something. She said little, and seemed to be forcing herself to smile now and then. Was she really Jonathan's mistress? Stella seemed so friendly towards her, chatting away to her, no sign of a sense of grievance. Ah well, sighed Kate to herself, the permissive society! She herself, she reflected a little sadly, didn't seem to get nearly as much out of it as most other people.

'Now then,' Stella cried to Kate as Jonathan poured her a drink, 'we want all the dirt.'

'There isn't yet anything much to tell. Wake gave a press conference with his inspector, the cheerful one, Sam Kippis.' She was thinking that Nellie Cordoni's hint that Stella was having an affair with Nick Bell must be merely gossip. Stella was not in the least perturbed that the man had been killed. Rather, it was an excitement. 'Sam Kippis did most of the talking, but he had precious little to say. They've no idea of motive. They've no suspects. They're not even sure at what time of the day Bell was killed, because—it's a bit gruesome—the heat of the sun on the greenhouse has thrown the medical evidence out of gear. Aside from the landlord of the Nag's Head, delivering the party drinks at about noon, they don't know of anyone who went to the house yesterday.'

She took a sip of her gin and watched Jonathan's face. He was well in control. There was no obvious change of expression, no look of relief. But she fancied there was a moment of fear in his eyes—or was it just fancy? 'Aside from the press conference,' she added, 'all I've done is talk to Mrs Cordoni.' She laughed. 'If even half

43

of what she says is true, village life around here makes our slice of Chelsea seem positively decorous. Provincial goings-on indeed!'

'She has a rare imagination,' said Jonathan. 'Come on, let's start lunch, or we'll be late.'

'It's the village flower show this afternoon,' explained Stella. 'Ever so sorry, but we'll have to desert you. Jon's running some of the sideshows, and Anne and I are helping in the tea tent. Of course, if you'd like to come along later, when it gets going . . .'

'We'd love to.'

'It's all rather comic. Best arrangement of three different vegetables, cottagers' class. Best home-made gooseberry wine. Egg-and-spoon race for children under eleven. All that sort of thing. A bit boring, but all the village turns up, and Rosa Hawkes, in her fanciest straw hat, makes a little speech and gives away the prizes. It's in the playing-field, just behind the church. Nothing much happens till about three, but if you two don't mind sitting around until then, you might care to look in. And Jon can at least crook the lucky dip for you.'

So after lunch they were alone together. Kate led the way on to the terrace, Henry following with the coffee-tray. They settled into deck-chairs.

'I gave Jonathan the advice he wanted about his mother's investment,' remarked Henry. 'He'd been a bit rash—taken a chance with a firm that's now about to go into liquidation. But luckily there's a cautionary clause put in by the old lady's solicitor that gives her a hold on the firm's chairman as guarantor. And he seems to be sound enough.'

'Good,' said Kate. 'How did you get on with the old ex-consul?'

He told her of the interview. When he came to the

blue rose, Kate crowed with joy. 'That's all I need for the piece I have to phone tomorrow. '

'Not the old boy's rose,' insisted Henry. 'I promised to keep quiet about that.'

'No, of course not. All I need is that Nick Bell had bred the first truly blue rose—and a hint that he may have been killed for it. Do you think there's any possibility it could be true?'

'There's one way of finding out. See if the rose plants are still in his garden, or whether they've been stolen.'

'How could you possibly tell among those hundreds of roses? Oh, I see. Obvious, really. Just by looking. If there are any bushes with blue roses on, they're still there. If not, somebody has swiped them.'

Henry shook his head. 'Too many possibilities of error. The blue rose bushes may not be blooming just at the moment, but may later. Then you won't know exactly what you're looking for. Old Hawkes's rose is pale blue. But what sort of blue had Bell produced? Had he in fact got a blue rose at all, or was it just another lavender shade? Was he lying when he said he had one—boasting? Nobody knows.'

'Presumably Dr Wisbech does.'

'Yes,' he conceded thoughtfully, 'presumably he does. But where does that get you? Suppose Wisbech is the chap we're looking for. Well, he's not a bad candidate. He has had a hand in breeding the rose. He and Bell quarrel. Perhaps he thinks Bell is trying to cheat him— pretend that the rose they bred in partnership isn't the blue one at all, but the blue was Bell's sole effort. Aside from prestige, there could be a share in £100,000 at stake. Wisbech is certainly a starter. So it's no use asking him to help identify the rose in Bell's garden. If we got a negative result, we wouldn't know whether it was true or false.'

'We must find out a bit more about Dr Wisbech,'

agreed Kate. 'Nellie Cordoni thought his wife was on drugs, and Bell was the supplier, but that's probably pure nonsense.'

'But there's another way we could find out if it's still there,' said Henry. 'All these rose hybridists keep meticulous and detailed records. Bell must have had a card index or something, corresponding with the code lettering on the labels on the roses themselves. It's a good bet the police haven't removed it. Why should they? So, if we could get back into Howth Lodge, we'd almost certainly find it. That should give us all the information we need to identify the rose in the garden.'

'Can we get back into the house? Have the police left it? Is it· locked? Who's looking after it?'

'I don't know, darling. But it won't be difficult to find out.'

Kate gave him the gist of what Nellie Cordoni had told her. Then she sat in silence for a while, sipping her coffee in the sunshine. 'Henry, I need your legal mind. I can't believe this fanciful rose business really stands up. It's much more likely to be over the women. Darling, sort out what we actually know.'

Henry considered. 'Very well. What happened at Howth Lodge yesterday that we are certain about?

'At some unknown time in the morning Mamie Barrington, the local alcoholic, went into the house—or, at any rate, into the garden. We don't know how long she was there, or whether Bell himself was there then, although he probably was. If he had been out, at any time, Mrs Cordoni would most likely have known, and told you. I place more credence on Mrs Cordoni, by the way, than you do. Most gossip is merely exaggerated fact. Now, what do we know about Mamie Barrington?'

'She's a drunk,' catalogued Kate, pulling a notebook from her handbag and beginning to tabulate all this in shorthand. 'She's the widow of a colonel who was killed in Malay. Her son Ralph, upon whom she dotes, is away at boarding school. According to Nellie, she's having an affair with Major Wilfred Sykes, who lives in Ashworth with his youngish, rather neurotic daughter Mary. You know, darling, that doesn't sound very probable to me. Why don't they marry, then? He's a widower.'

'Are you sure? Exactly—you don't know. He's probably married and separated from his wife. Have more faith in Nellie.'

'Okay. But that's all we know about Mamie Barrington, and it seems to have nothing whatever to do with Bell.'

'She went to Howth Lodge that morning. What time did she leave?'

'I don't know,' confessed Kate. 'I omitted to ask Nellie. All she said was, earlier than Mr Tooth delivering the booze. That makes it earlier than noon. Let's guess and say 11.00.'

'All right, but mark it a guess. Next thing that happens, at about noon Tooth delivers a crate of booze. Know anything about him?'

'Only that he's a gambler, loses a lot on the horses, Bell had baled him out some time earlier, and consequently is said to get his drink for free. And Tooth, still punting, has lost some more.'

'I think,' remarked Henry, 'you might put a circle round the name of Tooth. He's the nearest we've got yet to an ordinary, normal sort of motive.'

Kate nodded. 'Next thing that happens, about an hour later Sir Gerald drives up at his usual breakneck speed, brakes squeal, he goes into the lodge, emerges very quickly, and drives off. I've put that down at 13.00 hours. He probably went straight back to Rosa for his lunch. And the visit, so short, was probably just to say they'd turn up that evening. We don't know if he saw Bell. Later on, when we've got things a bit clearer, we could ask him.'

'Next,' Henry took up, 'Jonathan arrives in his old Austin car at about half past two.'

'14.30 hours,' noted Kate. 'He stays, according to Nellie, who is watching from her window seat, "quite a long time." Let's say half an hour. At 15.00 hours Nellie goes out to find him, to talk about the flower show, she says, but obviously out of curiosity to discover what he was doing. But before she gets to the gate, he hurries out, drives off, doesn't hear her call him. And she—so she says—doesn't go into the Lodge, but returns home. And he hasn't told the police he was there—that became clear at the press conference. Nobody called except Tooth, Kippis said.'

'I knew Jonathan pretty well when we were students,' said Henry slowly. 'I suppose I could imagine him as committing murder. He was always moody, rather contemptuous of society. On the other hand, he was never impetuous. And if we're to count him as a possible, it presumably has to be a quarrel because Bell had seduced his wife. Try to picture it. They're in Bell's greenhouse. He has been working at his roses. Jonathan shouts angrily about Stella. Bell makes some cynical remark. In a rage, Jonathan picks up the knife on the greenhouse bench and stabs Bell in the throat. Sound feasible to you?'

Kate shook her head. 'It's the Stella part I don't believe. I know you said she was flirting with Bell the last time you were here. But that could well have been mere party games. She doesn't seem at all thrown by his death. And she's such a normal, nice person. If she had been sleeping with him, it would have been because she imagined herself in love with the man. So she couldn't take his murder calmly. Then again, if it were true, she would know that Jonathan had found out and was in a rage. Even if she had no proof, she would suspect that Jonathan had killed him, so she would be in a dither of anxiety about that. And she isn't, Henry. At least, I don't think she is. She doesn't seem to me the sort of person who could hide all that away and act naturally.'

'I would accept all that, if Jonathan had disclosed to the police that he was at Howth Lodge yesterday afternoon. He's not an idiot. He must know what a terribly serious thing he's doing. So the reason for doing it must be very strong indeed. Whether he killed Bell or not, he certainly knows something he's trying to keep dark. If I had him under cross-examination, I doubt if he'd last ten minutes.'

Kate looked at her watch. 'We must go to their flower show soon. Let's make a quick summary. Let's assume there are two possible motives—the rose, or a woman. Rose first. Who?'

'It has to be an expert. There's Jack Clifford, the nurseryman. I suppose he must be counted as a possible, although we've absolutely nothing against him except that he's a rosarian.'

'And said to be in financial trouble,' put in Kate.

'All right. But who isn't these days? Then I suppose you ought to note down old Hawkes. He seems most unlikely, but he is a rosarian. And, of course, Dr Wisbech—on the face of it, the only really likely suspect.'

'Clifford, Sir Gerald and Dr Wisbech,' noted Kate. 'Now then, the list for the woman motive.'

'Jonathan, as we've agreed. Major Sykes, according to your gossip about Mamie Barrington. Clifford again, I suppose. He and his wife were there last evening.'

'According to Nellie, Clifford's wife wasn't one of Bell's conquests.'

'All right. But Nellie isn't infallible. Clifford does appear in both lists, with only a weak case against him in either. But the chap who may come out fairly strongly in both is Dr Wisbech. Some old stuff about his wife being on drugs, and Bell the supplier—presumably, by what we know of Bell, for his usual consideration.'

'Seems to me,' said Kate, shutting her notebook and getting ready to go, 'that being on both lists is a point in a suspect's favour. It's not very probable that somebody killed him because of both a rose and a woman.'

Henry agreed. 'But there's one point we've missed. All our suspects are men. Suppose it was a woman. No reason why a quick stab in the throat with a sharp knife shouldn't have been administered by a woman.'

'Two quick stabs,' amended Kate. But she opened her notebook again and wrote down, 'Mrs Clifford, Mamie Barrington, Mrs Wisbech, Stella.'

'How about Nellie herself? Suppose she hadn't been as unsusceptible as she claims. From her cottage, she's the one person who could most easily have gone to Howth Lodge without being noticed. And for all the other visits, except the publican's, all we've got is Nellie's unsupported word.'

Kate started to write down 'Mrs Cordoni.' Then she shut her notebook and laughed shortly. 'It's absurd, darling. We've written down practically every name in Ashworth that we know.'

A lane beside the church led to the recreation ground. On one side were parked cars; on the other, the children's races and competitions had begun; down the centre stretched a row of sideshows—hoopla, lucky dip, coconut shy, roll-the-penny and such—in aid of parish funds. The rector, a benign-looking old man in faded grey flannel suit and white straw hat, was chatting to various elderly women in ample summer frocks, and gazing with approval at the coins being raked in by the stallholders. Two big marquees at the far end housed the actual show of flowers and vegetables. From the loud-speaker on top of a small van blared dance music, slightly untuned. Jonathan, who was barking vigorously for the hoopla, the darts board and the coconut shy, waved cheerfully to them and accepted all the small coins in Henry's pocket, for Kate to miss wildly with darts, rubber rings and wooden balls in succession. 'Here, you try,' she commanded Henry, pointing to the untroubled coconuts on their iron stands. But he refused. 'The only way,' he told Jonathan, 'to maintain male superiority is never to try to prove it.'

It was pleasant inside the big marquees, sheltered from the strong breeze, the sunlight subdued, and natural colours and gentle fragrance from the flowers and carefully-arranged fruit and vegetables on the trestle tables. Villagers were drifting slowly round in small groups, peering at the red, blue and green cards pro-claiming the first, second and third prize-winners, in each class.

'The sedate, quiet, gentle life,' murmured Henry as they wandered round the first marquee. 'Why don't we lead it?'

'By all one hears of this village, we haven't sufficient erotic imagination,' answered Kate absently. She was trying to place the thick-set, middle-aged man in white linen jacket and grey slacks, peering at the prize-winners in the various classes of roses. Then she remembered. 'Good afternoon, Dr Wisbech.'

He looked round, unrecognizing; then his face dark-ened as he replied, 'Ah yes, last night, at poor Nicky's house. You were the girl who found him.'

'It was a fearful shock, even to us as strangers. How much worse it must be for all you people who knew him so well.'

51

'Dreadful,' he assented, but without, Kate thought, much conviction. 'A dreadful shock indeed.'

'I hear you collaborated with him in hybridizing roses.'

'Scarcely that. I sometimes supplied a little botanical information he needed. That was all.' He started to move away. 'A dreadful shock indeed.'

'Is Mrs Wisbech here?' asked Kate innocently.

He sent a quick glance into her eyes, then withdrew his gaze again. It was easy, of course, to imagine sinister expressions, Kate told herself, in such circumstances; all the same, his square-built, heavily-jowled face, dark of complexion, with one of those overhanging dark moustaches, had about it a sinister look—or perhaps furtive. Or, she told herself, perhaps only her imagination.

'No, my wife isn't here. She likes to rest in the afternoon. She is, I'm afraid, far from well.'

'I'm so sorry.'

'She suffers,' he said abruptly, 'from a rather difficult form of anaemia.'

Without any other word, he walked quite firmly away.

'Difficult man, I should say,' declared Henry. He began to read the names of the rose-classes prize-winning cards. 'Sir Gerald has done remarkably well. Almost scooped the pool.'

'How about the other rosarian?'

'Clifford? No, I can't see his name anywhere. Perhaps they don't allow professionals to enter. And I suppose Wisbech can't exhibit, because he doesn't live in the village.'

A florid, buxom woman standing beside him, told him: 'Seems awful not to see Mr Bell's name here. Every year he took most of the prizes—he and Sir Gerald between them, and Mr Bell usually came out top. And now he's been murdered. Nobody can take it in properly.

Here, in our own village, somebody murdered. Don't seem believable, somehow. First time I've really realized it is standing here, looking at the roses—and no prizes for Mr Bell.' She nodded to Henry and passed by. 'Awful!' she added.

'Dreadful!' he agreed.

They moved into the second tent, where the exhibits were mostly of village crafts—home-made wines, floral arrangements, cakes and tarts baked by the housewives, and home-made jams, junkets, lemon curd and cordials.

'Mrs Clifford's won quite a lot of prizes, anyhow,' observed Kate, moving from table to table. 'Baking, raspberry jam, elderberry wine . . .' As she turned back towards Henry, she saw Jack Clifford himself standing at the entrance to the tent. 'Hallo, Mr Clifford. Your wife has done well.'

'Yes, she always does,' he replied, but absently. He was not looking directly at Kate and was slightly swaying. He was not drunk, but had certainly been drinking. 'She's a splendid cook,' he declared. Then, looking suddenly at Kate: 'And she's a wonderful wife. We've been very happy.'

'I'm sure,' Kate soothed. He certainly did not look it. 'Where is Mrs Clifford?'

'She hasn't come. She was so upset by—by what happened yesterday, it has made her quite ill.' His gaze came round to Kate again. 'She's a very sensitive woman. She was dreadfully upset.'

'Would she like me to come to see her?'

'Oh, no,' he said in a vague voice, turning away. 'She doesn't take quickly to new people. She's a very shy woman. Kind of you, though. Very kind . . .' He drifted.

'What do you make of that?' Kate asked her husband.

'Nothing much, except that he's been drinking. But

53

didn't somebody tell us he's been on the bottle recently? So I don't make anything of it at all, except it makes me feel thirsty. Cup of tea?'

Already the tea tent was crowded. Stella had scarcely time to wave to them from behind the long table set with plates of cakes and sandwiches, thick white crockery and a huge enamel teapot from which Anne Brodie was rapidly pouring a steady stream of dark brown tea. 'Help yourself to milk and sugar,' Stella instructed Henry when he at last wedged his way to the table. 'Sandwiches and cakes further down, pay at the other end.'

He sidled gradually along the table, behind which were serving well-built village women in thin blouses and tweed skirts, sweating profusely under the artificial flowers and straw of their hats which none of them would dream of removing. Balancing plates and cups, he sidled his way to Kate and they went to sit on the grass outside.

Just as she was finishing her tea, gazing idly round, Kate suddenly stiffened. Henry asked, 'What has quickened your nose for news?'

She gestured to the far side of the stretch of grass along which the children's races were being run spasmodically. On a bench under a hawthorn tree, his brown trilby hat pulled a little over his eyes, sat Detective Chief Superintendent Wake.

'Quick,' she ordered Henry. 'Get me two more cups of tea, lots of sugar in one, and a plate of cakes and sandwiches.'

When he emerged, she took them from him and walked carefully round the knots of children and parents. She was fearful that, seeing her, he would get up and go away. But he smiled at her approach and stayed where he was.

'Hallo, Mr Wake. What brings you here, then?'

'Absorbing local atmosphere, let's say.'

'Care to absorb a cup of tea?'

'Bribing a police officer in the execution of his duty,' he said, 'and no bribe could be more acceptable. I hope you put in plenty of sugar.'

'You're not the first policeman I've met,' she told him, sitting on the bench beside him.

'And what have you come to ask me? You are the young woman from the *Post*, aren't you, who was enterprising enough to find the corpse?'

Kate nodded. 'And I haven't come to ask you anything, but to tell you something, on condition you don't tell anybody else until Monday, because it's my exclusive for the *Post* for Monday morning.'

'Not even Detective-Inspector Kippis?' he asked, faintly smiling.

'Specially not Detective-Inspector Kippis.'

'All right. What do you want to tell about?'

'A rose.'

Roger Wake's eyes came slowly round towards her, interested. 'You're a surprising young woman. I thought that, at most, you'd found the usual claimant eyewitness, or the routine maniac who confesses to the crime. But a rose—that could be something. So?'

'Bell was an amateur rose hybridist. There's a story that he bred a rather unusual rose, and a hint that he might have been murdered for it.'

'Who tells the story, and who gives the hint?'

'Reporters never reveal their sources of information.'

'So be it.'

After a pause, she asked, 'Do you think it too fanciful?'

'I learned long ago never to dismiss anything as impossible.'

'So you think that he was really killed because of a woman?'

'I don't think anything yet,' said Roger Wake. 'I have

55

simply started a police investigation, Mrs Theobald, and I shall try to assess the value of every fact that the investigation turns up, when it does.'

'Has it turned up much yet?'

'Information is always turning up, but as to its value or significance—that takes time to discover.'

'I told you about the rose,' she reminded him.

Wake smiled reluctantly. 'I don't usually like newspaper people. But you seem out of the usual. A confidence for a confidence, eh? All right—but this is completely off the record, not for publication. Somebody went to Howth Lodge yesterday who hasn't admitted it.'

Kate stared at him. 'You're trying to use me, aren't you, Mr Wake?'

'Yes,' he allowed, 'I am. It may be insignificant or it may be very important indeed. The way you nose around, you might stumble across it before we do. If you do, come and tell me or Kippis—or Bates, or any policeman you can find—without a moment's delay. I mean that. If it is significant, it is almost certainly dangerous. Don't try any follow-up on your own, Mrs Theobald. There might be risks of which you know nothing.'

CHAPTER VI

THEY ARGUED about it all the way to the pub. After supper Jonathan had taken Anne Brodie back to the university for a Philological Society party, he said; and Stella, apologizing for their shortcomings as hosts, had admitted to a pounding headache from the heat and noise of the tea tent and taken herself to bed. Not to worry, Henry had assured her. He and Kate would be happy to stroll off to the village pub for a couple of drinks, and then turn in themselves. Gratefully, Stella handed him the front-door key.

So all the way to the pub they argued about it. After what Roger Wake had said to Kate at the flower show, Henry maintained it was imperative to tell him that Jonathan had been at Howth Lodge the previous afternoon. But Kate was reluctant. 'Quite apart from the practical difficulty,' she argued, 'that we'd have to turn out of the Old Rectory and find a bed somewhere else—and there isn't one for miles—I'm not at all sure how much Wake already knows and is not disclosing to me. What he said was that somebody went there yesterday and hasn't admitted it. So he knows that somebody was there.'

'And obviously doesn't know who it was.'

'But darling, we know of four people who were there yesterday—Mamie Barrington, Sir Gerald and the landlord of the Nag's Head, as well as Jonathan. Do you reckon that Wake knows that too? He must, with Nellie Cordoni around.'

Henry shrugged.

'Then what's he up to,' Kate went on, 'talking of only one person? The more I think of it, the more I believe he was just saying anything, to fob me off. He notoriously dislikes newspaper people. And all that stuff about it being dangerous not to tell him at once. Why should it be dangerous?'

'Not unreasonable, darling. There's somebody around here who was damn dangerous for Nick Bell yesterday. Having committed one murder, why should he hesitate at a second, to cover up?'

'Oh, bosh!' exclaimed Kate—but not very convincingly, even to herself.

Once they reached the Nag's Head they had to drop the argument. The bar was crammed with newspapermen, all drinking heavily on expenses and buying drinks for the few locals who had come in, ready to invent anything for a couple of pints. The saloon was small and very old—exposed oak beams everywhere, an open hearth with an ancient oak bressummer and artificial flowers thrust among the andirons and suspended from the pothooks; the bar itself of beer-stained oak worn smooth for centuries. The landlord was busily serving behind it, helped by a lean woman who was evidently his wife, and a moon-faced girl pulling the beerhandles.

While Henry was shoving up to the bar to get a beer, and a scotch for Kate, she spotted Dereck Andrews sitting by himself over a mug at the far end of the room. She struggled across to greet him and he made place for her on the bench. 'Let me get you a drink.'

'Henry's getting them.'

'Anything special I can use tomorrow?' he asked. 'I've got to phone in the next half-hour.'

'Only what I'm saving for my own piece on Monday. How's the book going?'

He brightened at that and began a detailed account of his latest study of 'Breath,' scarcely pausing to nod to Henry when he arrived with the drinks. After a time he looked at his watch and remarked he had better go and scribble something for the main edition.

'If it's any use to you,' volunteered Kate, 'I can give you details of the inside of the house, and the greenhouse where the body was.'

'Thanks, but I've seen it.'

'Aren't the police still there?' asked Henry, surprised.

'They locked the place up and left at mid-day. What they don't know is that there's an old charwoman in the village, who used to clean for Bell, who has a key.'

'Surely the village constable knows that.'

'No doubt. But one of the county men snubbed him, so he's sulking. Says he's clearly not wanted where the big boys are, so he'd better stay away and get on with his normal duties.'

'Who's the old charwoman, and where does she live?' asked Kate.

'Mrs Lovell. No. 2, Bridge Cottages. She lets out the key for £1 an hour. Don't pay more or you'll spoil the market. But it's only the key to the house. You can't get through to the greenhouse—the garden wall is high and topped with broken glass, the door in the wall is locked, and Mrs Lovell doesn't have a key to that. But you don't need it. Turn right down the second lane past the church, coming from this direction. After about half a mile, a cart track goes off to the left. This leads to the back of Bell's paddock, where he planted out a lot of his roses—but, of course, you know that. There's only a wooden fence to get over, and one of the lads has snipped a gap in the barbed wire on top. There is a gate, but that's locked too. The greenhouse is also locked, but, of course, you can see into it. Only the roof lights are shaded with blinds. But why do you want to get in? You've already seen it all.'

'One never knows,' said Kate. Dereck nodded and made off upstairs to his room.

Henry supped his beer and gazed comfortably round at the pleasant scene—nothing he liked better than a country pub on a Saturday night. 'Landlord doesn't seem too happy,' he remarked, 'in spite of all the trade.'

'He's a miserable sod,' chipped in the man sitting just behind him. 'But what can you expect? He used to be a comic.'

Swivelling, Kate greeted this second reporter: 'Hallo Fred. Didn't see you sitting there. This is Henry, my old man.' The two men nodded. 'How do you mean, he used to be a comic?'

'Variety act. Billy Tooth. He had a grotty blonde as partner and they tried to model themselves on Burns and Allen. Billy and Belle, the act was. But they weren't much good. They got on television a few times, then faded. I don't know what happened to Belle. Went back to the old trade, probably. But Billy Tooth married the landlord's daughter in this pub. That's her—the grim-looking bitch behind the bar, name of Emily. When her father died, Billy and Emily took over the pub. Don't know what the hell he's got to be miserable about. It must be better than a third-rate variety act, traipsing round working men's clubs in Lancashire.'

'I heard he plays the horses and has lost a lot,' said Kate, 'and Bell helped him with his gambling debts.'

Fred nodded approvingly at her. 'You got on to that too, did you? I've put it rather prominently into my piece for tomorrow. Well, there's got to be some sort of hint of a suspect. And what else do we know? Damn-all.'

'Where does the suspicion come in?'

'He's up to his ears in debt. Bookies can turn very nasty to them what don't pay. Billy Tooth was at Howth Lodge that morning. And there was supposed to be a lot of cash kept there.'

'Kippis said so—£300 in a cashbox in a locked cupboard in the dining-room. But it wasn't touched.'

'How do we know there wasn't other money there? Well, all right, I know it's a bit thin. I couldn't risk more than the slightest hint. You try to do better.'

'I will that, Fred,' she promised him. 'Luckily I've got all Sunday before I have to put in my effort.'

'Another drink, Fred?' asked Henry.

'No thanks, old man. I'd better go and phone a bit more for the later editions. See you.'

When he had gone, they sat lazily sipping a second drink, not talking much, relaxing. At last he put down his tankard and said, 'How about off?' And Kate nodded.

Away from the pub the village street was silent, with no sign of life except a glow behind a window curtain in one cottage or another. A bright round moon had splendidly risen above the dark silhouette of a row of ancient elms, so that the scene was softly but charmingly lit, every shadow a detail.

Henry put his arm round her as they wandered up the street.

'About Jonathan,' she said dreamily. 'Let's not decide anything tonight, eh? Plenty of time to think it out in the morning.'

Henry nodded, turned her towards him and kissed her. Kate sighed, gazing at the moonlit street, 'It's romantic enough even for husbands.'

As they turned into the garden of the Old Rectory, Henry said quietly, 'On the subject of husbands, and wives . . .'

Kate kissed him warmly, feeling for the strength of his shoulders beneath his jacket. 'Let's not change the subject.'

Much later, as the moonlight peered into the room and on to the rumpled bed where she lay in his arms, satisfied and happy, Kate suddenly began to giggle.

'What is it now?' asked Henry dreamily.

'Sorry, darling. It just came into my head. Rabbie Burns and a' that. O my luve is like a red, red rose . . .'

Henry kissed her lazily on the mouth, and pinched her gently on the bottom. 'Aren't you the incorrigible woman! Go to sleep.'

In the morning, Kate said, 'Mrs Lovell, the obliging charwoman. No. 2, Bridge Cottages. And the going rate for the key is £1 an hour. Will you collect it, darling?'

Henry, towelling his hair after his bath, asked, 'Why do you want to go back there?'

'The blue rose, of course. It was you who said there must be some sort of code index, so that we could identify it in the garden or the greenhouse. Before I write my piece for tomorrow's paper, I'd like to see whether the plants are still there or not.'

'Okay. Whatever you say. I'm only the reporter's apprentice.'

Kate drove to the village shop and bought all the Sunday papers. The Ashworth murder was not prominent in any of them, chiefly because none of the crime men had anything very exciting to reveal. With a nod of satisfaction at the open field for her own piece next day, she threw the newspapers on to the back seat of the car and went on to Howth Lodge.

Henry was waiting outside with the key. 'That old woman's making a fortune. She has upped the rate to £1.50.'

'Don't look back,' warned Kate as they went on. 'Nellie Cordoni's certainly watching from her windowbox. But, after all, she must have seen the entire newspaper press of the country going in during the last 24 hours.'

Inside the house it was peculiarly silent, as though the idea of death were still there. The rooms were dark because the curtains had been left drawn. Henry switched on a lamp, assuring Kate the light would not be seen from outside against daylight.

He produced two pairs of thin rubber gloves. 'With the police registering fingerprints, better be cautious.'

The obvious place to start was a desk in one corner of the living-room. It was not locked. But its drawers contained nothing remotely like an index of roses; only neat dockets of receipted bills and carefully rubber-banded cheque stubs. There were some correspondence files, too, over which Kate could have wished to linger, but Henry drove her on; they had not come for that.

They moved to the dining-room. Here was the cupboard in which the cashbox had been kept. The cupboard was now unlocked. The police had, of course removed the cashbox. Henry, lifting a chair over, climbed up to inspect the upper shelves. He reported there were only files of correspondence, a large number of back copies of a botanical magazine, and an old typewriter. Kate, at the lower shelves, was equally disappointed—a great many old newspapers, seemingly unmarked and in no sort of sequence. Bell seemed to have had the habit of throwing old newspapers into this cupboard. In the bottom there was a crate containing half-a-dozen bottles of V.S.O.P. cognac. But no index of roses.

'Let's try upstairs,' she suggested.

There were only two bedrooms. The smaller was bare of anything except plain furniture and seemed to have been little used. The other room was large. In the middle, backed against the wall, stood a huge four-poster bed. 'Equipment,' murmured Henry, 'for Mr Bell's other hobby.' He opened a carved oak armoire. 'And here's some more.' Hanging there were lengths of scarlet silk rope, a jewelled dog-collar, a couple of short leather whips and a transparent plastic mackintosh. At the bottom, leaning against the side, was a small bundle of thin canes. He picked one up to inspect. At one end was the dark stain of blood. 'Not a very nice man, the late Mr Bell,' he commented, shutting the armoire door.

Kate had wandered over to a mahogany dressing chest standing beneath the windowsill. It was a charming piece, obviously 18th-century. What puzzled her was that there was something familiar about it. She pulled the brass handles of the top drawer. A writing table slid out. Then she remembered. 'Father had one of these, Henry. It had a secret drawer.' She slid the green baize writing-surface back to reveal a dressing-mirror that hinged upwards, flanked by four rosewood compartments with beauti-fully-fitting lids. She groped around the compartments, trying to make her fingers remember. Suddenly a flap clicked open. She lifted it to find the secret compartment beneath.

Henry came across. 'Any luck?'

'No. Only a bundle of letters and a clipping from some old newspaper.'

'Ah well, there's no reason why he should have kept his rose index in a secret place.' He checked suddenly. 'What idiots we are. What are we looking for? Not necessarily a card index—more likely a sort of studbook. And where's the obvious place to keep a book? On a bookshelf. One wall of the living-room is all books, and there are more shelves in the entrance hall. Come on, that's where we'll find it.'

'You go on,' she told him. 'I've got to remember how to fiddle this thing shut.'

When he had gone, Kate quickly whipped the bundle of letters and the newspaper clip into her handbag. If they were Bell's secrets, she wanted to know them. She pressed the lid of the secret compartment into place, lowered the mirror, slid out the green baize top and pushed the whole drawer back. Before she left, she glanced into the two other drawers of the chest. They contained only shirts and underclothes.

'Here they are,' called Henry as she descended the stairs. He was standing in the living-room near the fireplace, where the biggest arm-chair was placed. In his hand he held a large, leather-bound book that looked like a ledger. 'This was obviously Bell's favourite chair. All the shelves within arm's reach are rose textbooks. And here are his 3 studbooks. They seem to be in sequence, with a lot of cross-reference from one to the other.'

He examined a few pages carefully, then turned up the references in the second book. 'I think I get it. First the pedigrees of the parent roses he started with, 7 years ago. Then he cross-bred a lot of his own hybrids, so you have to keep referring back to get the full pedigree of any one plant. The end column gives letters and numbers for each plant—the code, I think, for where it is in the garden. Snag is, we need a key to the garden lay-out.'

He picked up the third volume. A folded sheet of stout paper fell out. 'Ah, here it is. A plan of the rose beds in the garden and the paddock, with the coding against each row and position. Let's try one at random. Here's a rose he called "Starlight. Seedling (see Vol. i, page 138) x Sutter's Gold. Yellow shaded amber and pink, with yellow reverse." That must be its pedigree and description—it's a simple one, most are very much more complicated. Now, in the end column, the code PB 3/5. He turned to the plan. 'Yes, here's the P group, row B. Presumably it's position No. 3, and there are 5 plants.'

'What it is,' sighed Kate, 'to possess a logical mind!'

'All right. But what do we do now? I can't possibly study these books here. It would take hours.'

'So we take them with us.'

'But we can't,' he protested.

'Of course we can. We'll put them back when we've finished with them. What harm can that do?' She found an opaque plastic carrier in the kitchen. 'They'll fit into this, so even Nellie Cordoni won't know what we've got. Better make sure, by the way, that we've got everything.' She went to the shelf from which the pedigree books had come. The next was a clothbound manuscript book. 'Do we need this?'

Henry opened it. 'Indeed we do. Good job you looked. It's the index of all the rose names, telling where to find them in the pedigree books.'

Before they left the cottage he slung his jacket over his arm, hiding the plastic carrier from sight. 'You always underrate Nellie,' he said. 'I'd rather she didn't know we had taken anything.'

After Kate dropped him off in the village, Henry returned the key to Mrs Lovell, slipping her an extra 50p.

as sweetener (bearing in mind that he would need the key again to return the books, and there must not be a slip-up). He walked back to the Old Rectory. The hired car was parked in the drive. Stella and Jonathan were already seated on the back terrace with gins and tonic. As Henry approached, Anne Brodie came out to join them. 'Kate's gone upstairs to freshen,' Stella called to him.

'Thanks. I will too. Have you completely recovered?'

'Oh yes, thanks. It was only a headache—the heat in the tea tent, and all those cackling old women.'

Kate was seated by the bedroom window, waiting for him. She had brought the books upstairs without being noticed, she told him. They were locked in his suitcase. He promised to get down to them after lunch.

On the terrace Jonathan poured drinks while they chattered.

'Did you have a good party?' Henry asked Anne.

'Oh, the usual undergraduate thing, with a smattering of younger dons, such as Jon.'

'Were you plotting a sit-in?'

She laughed. First time, he thought, he had seen the girl laugh, or even raise much more than a faint smile. 'Oh no, just a drink-in.'

'What would you like to do this afternoon?' asked Jonathan.

'We're terribly unsatisfactory hosts,' said Stella. 'We've neglected you appallingly.'

'On the contrary,' Henry declared, 'it's wonderful to be left alone to do what you like. It's much more onerous being a guest than a host.'

'What Henry means,' explained his wife, 'is that he likes a short nap on his bed of a Sunday afternoon—about a couple of hours, usually.'

'Suits us,' said Jonathan.

'Trouble is,' went on Kate, 'I've got to write my piece

for the *Post*, without disturbing my lord's sleep. Is there some small room where I won't be in the way?'

'My dear girl,' Jonathan told her, 'this vast house is full of huge, empty rooms where nobody ever goes. Take your pick. Want to borrow a typewriter?'

'That would be a help.'

So after lunch Henry went up to the bedroom with a perfectly accepted excuse, unlocked his suitcase and settled by the window to study the books of pedigrees of Nicholas Bell's roses. Within half an hour he nearly was asleep. Not only were the pedigrees, with all their cross-referencing, extremely complicated, but to a non-rosarian extremely tedious. 'Iceberg x Pink Parfait' or 'Josephine Bruce x Pink Peace', and so on, were nothing to him but sets of undescriptive words. Even the brief descriptions that followed of seedling offspring did not form pictures for him. If he were expert enough to know what the named roses looked like, it would have been a different matter, he was sure. As it was, it was no more evocative than reading names from a telephone directory.

He persevered, however, for nearly another hour. Then he gave it up. By then, he realized, he was reading the words without conveying anything to his mind at all. Moreover it had become clear that identifying the rose he was seeking was mere chance, because he wasn't certain exactly what he was looking for. Somewhere, no doubt, in those hundreds of pages of complicated rose pedigrees, written in ink in a small, neat hand, was the identification of the blue rose. He might well search for hours before finding it. Indeed, he might read right through the books and not find it at all, for his concentration was getting patchy, so that he could easily read the description without taking it in; possibly had already done so.

There must, he pondered, be some other approach. The most promising was through the small fourth volume, the index to the three others. But this was useless unless he knew the name of the rose he was trying to find. The index was only of rose names, without descriptions. Bell himself, of course, needed nothing more. As an expert he would know all the parent roses by name, and the new names were those he had himself given to his seedlings; or at least, Henry supposed, to those which had passed successfully through the first two or three stages of development—a minority only. He could not have named all the thousands which he raised, and often speedily discarded.

Henry gazed out of the bedroom window at the dark shrubberies of the Old Rectory garden. To use these books he had to discover, from some other source, the name that Bell had given to his blue rose.

Who would be likely to know it? Dr Wisbech certainly would, as Bell's partner in the enterprise. But he could not be questioned. The man was full enough of suspicion already. If he found somebody prodding about among the roses he and Bell had raised together, he would make an obvious deduction. So that if he were in fact the man they were looking for, it would simply be warning him well in advance, giving him time to destroy the chances of proof.

Jack Clifford, the rose nurseryman, might well know. Marketing a new rose must need professional organization, and the obvious man to whom Bell could have turned was Clifford. So Clifford could be asked—but preferably rather early in the morning, before the day's drinking had set in.

The only other possible was Sir Gerald Hawkes. He was less likely to know the name, but a lot easier to approach.

Henry went downstairs into the hall. He looked around the house but could see nobody. So he found Sir Gerald's number and dialled it. The old man himself answered.

'Oh, hallo Sir Gerald. Hope I'm not disturbing your siesta.'

Sir Gerald cackled agreeably. 'Haven't had one since we came home from Lima, my dear young man. What can I do for you?'

'One thing I should have asked you yesterday, my wife tells me. Afraid I'm not a very competent reporter. Do you happen to know if Bell had given his blue rose a name?'

'He was going to, but I'm not sure whether he actually did. He bred it from one of his own seedlings as female parent, with a rose species only a few generations back in its pedigree, I believe—a stroke of genius, that. For the male parent he used Baby Faurax. He told me that when I told him that one of the parents I was using was Lilac Charm. Of course, both pieces of information were valueless unless you knew, and indeed possessed a specimen of the other parent in either case.'

'Did he tell you what he was proposing to call his blue rose?'

'Oh yes. Stella Sims—in honour of your present hostess.'

Henry stood in silence for a moment, then gathered himself sufficiently to thank Sir Gerald and put down the phone.

Then he went in search of Kate.

He found her at last, seated at a round library table covered with a typewriter and a jumble of papers, in a room lined with empty bookshelves.

He gave her what Sir Gerald had told him. 'So that settles it,' he said. 'We must now tell the police that Jonathan was at Howth Lodge on Friday.'

'Aren't you making a rather large assumption?' she asked slowly.

'I don't know whether it's valid or not. But you must admit that there's now more than a possibility.'

Kate considered. 'Why don't we challenge Jonathan direct? After all, Henry, we are his guests. If we're going to the police with information about him, I think we ought to tell him first.'

'The Superintendent warned you against trying a follow-up on your own.'

'Oh, nonsense. I don't for a moment believe there's any kind of risk.' She smiled at him with sweet sarcasm. 'Even if there were, I've got you to protect me, darling.'

It was supper time before they could get hold of Jonathan. He came in a bit earlier, but then Kate was engrossed with phoning her story to the *Post*.

'They were pleased with it,' she reported to Henry. 'The blue rose thing makes it. There wasn't much in the Sundays about our murder, because the boys hadn't got much. But now, Butch says, the blue rose murder is well and truly on page one. And Kate is the bright girl. So that's all right.'

They waited until after supper. Then Kate helped Stella clear the table and start the washing-up in the kitchen, and Henry began on Jonathan: 'We're in a damned awkward situation, and Kate and I have agreed that the only way is to be quite frank with you. It's about Bell's murder. You went to Howth Lodge about half past two on Friday afternoon.'

Jonathan, lighting his pipe, regarded him calmly. 'Yes, I did.'

'You stayed for about half an hour.'

'Nellie Cordoni is an accurate observer.'

'Did you see Bell?'

'No, he wasn't there. At least, he wasn't in the house. It didn't occur to me to look in the greenhouse.'

'Why did you stay so long?'

'I wanted to see him, and I hoped he'd come in. He

isn't usually out for long. So I waited. There was something I wanted to talk to him about rather urgently.'

'About Stella?'

'Stella?' He took his pipe from his mouth and stared, apparently astonished. Then he suddenly laughed. 'So that's what you think.' He walked quickly over to the door and shouted: 'Stella. I'm having a chat with Henry, and I think you ought to be in on it. Have you girls finished washing-up? Then please come and join us. It's rather funny.'

The two women came in, Stella rolling down the sleeves of her cardigan and lighting a cigarette. 'What is it?'

'Henry knows that I was at Nick Bell's place on Friday afternoon.'

'Were you, Jon?' There was anxiety in the question. Clearly Stella had not known. 'Why?'

'Henry thinks it was because I'd discovered that you and Nicky were having it off, so I went up there to stick a knife in him. Isn't that what you think, Henry?'

'Not necessarily. But I do think, as they say in my trade, there's a case to answer. I suppose you know that Bell had bred a rose which he expected to become famous, and he had named it Stella Sims.'

'Of course I know.' For the first time Jonathan was looking angry. 'It was a nice gesture to his friends. He asked our permission for the name. It doesn't have any dirty connotation.'

Kate said: 'Let's be sensible. Sit down everybody. Now then, let me tell it. According to Nellie Cordoni, at least three people went to Howth Lodge on Friday, not counting the publican who delivered the drinks. Mrs Barrington, Sir Gerald Hawkes very briefly and you Jonathan. She says you stayed about half an hour, then came out and drove off quickly.'

'And Nellie also told you, no doubt, that Stella was

having an affair with Nick Bell. And the named rose seemed to you both to confirm it. Why don't you ask Stella if it was true? I know, of course, that it wasn't. This place reels with gossip, Kate, just as the university does down the road. It's equally asserted there that I'm bedding down with Anne. In fact, I'm not. The truth is that Anne is somebody both Stella and I are very fond of, and we've taken her under our wing. She also happens to be a poet of quite unusual strength, and may become a considerable writer. She's an awkward, shy person, and doesn't get on well at Wessex. It's a long story—parents' broken marriage, childhood incidents that warped her attitude to sex, every damned sort of inhibition that's likely to break down into excesses. We thought that if she'd a couple of friends to talk to about it all, she'd miss the worst.' His eyes darkened. 'We were wrong,' he added abruptly.

Suddenly his wife came in with the same question as before: 'Why did you go there, Jon?'

His sallow face darkened. He hesitated for a moment, then answered in a mutter, 'To warn him off Anne. He had corrupted her.'

'Oh, no!'

'I found out by accident.' He turned to Kate. 'So I went with just the sort of motive you imagined, but over a different woman.'

'What did you say to him?' asked Stella.

'I didn't see him. I waited for some time, but he didn't come in. I suppose he was already dead, out in the greenhouse—I don't know.' He turned to Kate again. 'I assure you that, if I had seen him, I should have been capable, that afternoon, of killing him. His sexual habits were unprepossessing.'

'There's just one other thing, Jonathan,' said Kate. 'Why did you conceal from the police that you had gone there?'

'Conceal from the police? Do you think I'm as stupid as that? Of course I didn't. I told young Bates on Friday evening. To put my motives no higher, if I hadn't, I knew perfectly well that Nellie Cordoni would. I knew she'd seen me.'

'Then the whole thing's a mare's nest,' said Henry, immensely relieved. 'My dear chap, I am sorry. But we felt we had to put it to you.'

'Wait a minute,' objected Kate. 'At the police conference on Saturday morning somebody put the direct question—did the police know of anybody who had been at Howth Lodge on Friday, before the drinks party? And Kippis said, only the landlord of the Nag's Head.'

'I'm not surprised. Bates went to see his boss, that fellow Wake, and came back to ask me not to tell anybody I'd been there. He said something about somebody else having been there, and they didn't want to scare that person off, or something. I don't know. My dear Kate, you don't have to believe me. Simply ask Kippis or Wake, or whoever you newspaper people see tomorrow morning.'

Kate looked at him hard for a moment, then smiled broadly. 'I can't tell you what a relief it is. Of course I believe you.' She turned to Stella. 'My dear Stella, we've been so anxious. Forgive us?'

'Nothing to forgive. I'm grateful to you both for coming out with it.'

She still looked, thought Kate, disturbed, as though from shock. She was pale, and there was none of the usual cheerfulness to her.

'So now it's all over, let's forget it,' said Kate.

'Let's have a drink,' said Jonathan abruptly. 'Scotch for you two?'

They had three rounds before they went to bed. What puzzled Henry was that something was still troubling

Kate. The others would not notice it, but Henry knew she was unsatisfied about something.

As he closed the bedroom door behind him, he asked, 'What is it, darling?'

'I'm not sure. Somehow, everything doesn't seem quite to fit.'

When they were in bed and he had switched off the light, she suddenly said, 'Obviously Roger Wake wasn't referring to Jonathan when he spoke of somebody who hadn't admitted going to the house. Then who?'

CHAPTER VII

DERECK ANDREWS telephoned the Old Rectory early on Monday morning to tell Kate that Inspector Kippis was to be available at Linchester police station at 10.30.

'That was a good piece you had in the *Post* this morning, Kate. Several of the lads who were going back to London have had frantic messages from their offices to stay on. I'm going back this evening, but if the story's still running by Thursday, we'll be here again for the Sundays. So keep it going, there's a good girl.'

'Do my best, dear.'

'You'll have to find something other than the blue rose. All the boys are worrying that one to death this morning. We shall rely on you to bring us something fresh every day, dear Kate. We can all do with a few days in the country—it's damn hot in London.'

She left Henry to his study of Bell's pedigree books and drove into Linchester. There was no entry under the name Stella Sims in the index. Probably, Henry said, he hadn't got round to it yet. But Henry was confident he could identify the blue rose from Sir Gerald's reference to its parents. 'There are a lot of entries under Baby Faurax. Bell often used it as parent. I simply have to go through them all until I find a cross with one of Bell's own seedlings.'

'Won't there probably be several?'

'I expect so. But I have one other clue. The seedling has a rose species only a few generations back in its pedigree. According to Sir Gerald, that's very unusual —a stroke of genius on Bell's part, he called it. So if I put on a wet towel and trace through all pedigrees of seedlings crossed with Baby Faurax, I should be able to get the right one.'

'No reporter should be without a spouse with legal training,' she told him, kissing him and setting off for Linchester.

Directly she turned into the police park, Horace came loping over with his grievance. 'Is that your idea of working together? Damn it, Kate, you had the best story of the lot, and didn't even give me a hint of it. So I look like a bloody fool to the office, turning in pix of villagers, and the village main street, and not a bloody rose in sight. Why didn't you tip me off?'

'Didn't see you. You should keep in touch, Horace.' The real reason she hadn't tipped him off was that she had suffered from Horace of old. He would have gone round the Nag's Head boasting that he had an exclusive, old man. Within half an hour somebody would have got it out of him. Tell Horace? Not much!

'I was in touch with the office,' he grumbled. 'Isn't that good enough?'

'Sure it is,' she replied, making for the station door. 'They knew all about it at the office. They had my full story by early evening. I'm surprised they didn't tell you, Horace.'

'What a bloody newspaper to work for! I ought to go back to an agency.'

'We'd miss you,' she told him. 'We'd certainly miss you.'

She took a good-natured barracking from the others when she pushed into the back room of the police station. Give the lady a blue rose. A rose by any other colour would smell as fishy. And so on. But there was respect in it. Kippis and young Bates took the seats behind the desk—no sign this time of Wake. Kippis at once joined in. 'I think we ought to ask Mrs Theobald to take the conference. How about that? She knows a lot more than we do.'

'Just a little girl trying to get along,' murmured Kate demurely.

Kippis grinned and turned to business. 'But the fact is, we really don't know much yet. All I can tell you today is that we have had the pathologist's report and there are one or two interesting things in it. Bell was certainly killed where his body was found. It was fairly obvious from the start, because of the blood, but there was a slight possibility that he had been killed elsewhere and moved to the greenhouse. That's now ruled out. The time of death remains a bit uncertain, because of the greenhouse conditions, as I told you on Saturday. It was during daylight hours that day, and probably around the middle of the day. The other point of interest to come out of the medical report is that we now have to look for the murder weapon.'

'But it was in his throat,' interjected someone.

Kippis shook his head. 'That's just it. The knife that was in the wound was not the weapon with which he was killed.'

He raised his hand to quieten the sudden, startled buzz of comment. 'Just a minute, please. This is a bit complicated. Let me go through it without interruption, or you'll throw me. Questions afterwards, if you like.

'Now then. The knife in the wound—which I'm told

76

is not technically a pruning knife, but a grafting knife—that's just a note for you horticultural experts—had been inserted only to the length of the blade. That blade is approximately 3 inches long. The wound penetrates the righthand side of the throat, pierces the artery and one of the jugular veins, and the gullet, and continues into the lefthand side of the throat to a total depth of $3\frac{1}{2}$ inches. So it couldn't have been made by a 3-inch blade.

'No, wait a minute, don't interrupt. There are two other indications that the grafting knife was not the murder weapon. The blade of the grafting knife is quite an appreciable bit narrower than the wound. That, of course, isn't conclusive. A cut could have been made much wider than the actual blade. But, taken with the second factor, it's indicative.

'The second factor is that only one edge of the grafting knife is sharp. The other is blunt, because the blade folds away into the handle, like any ordinary pocket-knife. The grafting knife was found in the wound with the sharp edge forward, facing towards the corpse's front. But, as you know, there was another gash, on the front of the throat, so that the murderer appears to have struck twice. But, in order to make that gash on the front of the throat, the sharp edge of the knife would have had to be facing backwards.

'Now, I suppose it's just possible that whoever used the knife held it in the hand with the blade facing backwards for the first blow, and quickly twisted the knife in the hand so that the blade faced forwards for the second blow. But it doesn't seem very likely. So, taking all three factors into consideration—the depth of the wound, the width of the wound, and the position of the other gash on the throat—it seems reasonably certain that the murder was not committed with a knife-blade with only one sharp edge, and quite certain that it was not committed with the knife found in the wound.'

Then the questions broke. Kippis let them run for a couple of minutes before raising his hand again. 'What it boils down to, of course, is firstly, why was the grafting knife put into the wound after Bell had been killed with some other weapon, and, secondly, what kind of other weapon?

'Now, nobody may attribute any of this to us. No police-spokesman stuff, or anything of that kind. At this stage it's as much speculation on our part as on yours. But if you want background guidance on what we think may have happened, then the answer to the first question would be something like this. The murderer killed Bell with his own weapon—or, of course, her own weapon, for the blow was well within the capability of a woman. The angle of the wound suggests that, when the killing blow was struck, Bell had half turned his back on the other person. So he would not have seen the blow coming, and the murderer would not have had to contend with any defensive movement by Bell himself. Now, wait a minute, George. I can guess the question you're going to ask, and it's a good one. But let me finish first. When Bell had been killed, the murderer realized that the weapon would identify him. So he substituted one of several of Bell's own gardening knives that were lying on the greenhouse workbench, and took his own weapon away. Now George, your question . . .'

'You say that the blow that killed Bell was struck when his back was half turned, so that he didn't see it coming. But he was killed by the second of two blows—and the first was on the front of his throat.'

Kippis nodded approvingly. 'As I said, a good question. Mind you, you're making one assumption that is not necessarily true. We can't be certain that the gash on the front of the throat was not made as a second blow, after Bell had been killed. But I agree that it seems unlikely.

'So we have to ask how Bell could have been gashed on the front of the throat by a blow he must have seen coming, and why he then obligingly turned his back ready for the killing blow, and made no attempt to defend himself. The most likely answer that we can find at the moment is that, in fact, there was only one blow.'

'Oh, come on, Inspector,' cried somebody. 'Don't give it to us in riddles.'

Kippis grinned. 'Okay. We think that one blow was struck by a double-bladed weapon. One blade caught the front of his throat, and the other penetrated the side, and killed him.

'The kind of weapon would be a one-handed grass shears, for example. And that's most likely what it was. You know the thing—two blades, like big scissors blades, joined by a spring handle which you grasp in one hand, usually to trim the edges of lawns, or the grass round trees and so on. The most usual ones have blades about $4\frac{1}{2}$ inches long, and considerably wider than the blade of a grafting knife. So, for your background information only, that's the kind of weapon we're looking for.'

'Do you mean we can't use it?'

'Use it by all means. It will be useful to have the village looking for a pair of one-handed grass shears thrown away somewhere, or maybe hidden. And we'd very much like to know if anybody is missing any garden implement like that. But don't attribute any of it to us, please. It's going to be a difficult weapon to find—there must be one in every garden shed in the district.'

'Are you searching the garden sheds, then?'

'No comment.'

'Any idea of motive yet?'

'Didn't the *Post* tell us it was either a rose or a woman? Now it has opted for the rose—blue variety.'

Kate readily joined the laugh. The meeting continued

for another quarter of an hour, by which time it was clear that Kippis wasn't going any further that day, and the reporters started to disperse.

She drove back to the Old Rectory. Stella was just getting into her own car with a shopping basket. 'I'm going into Linchester for a lunch date with a girl in the town. Will you two be all right on your own? There's plenty of food in the fridge. Jon'll be at the university all day—Mondays are busy for him.'

'Don't worry about us. I'm afraid we're being a damn nuisance. Would it be easier if we moved into a pub somewhere?'

'Don't think of it. As long as you don't mind fending for yourselves a good deal of the time, it's lovely to have you. You help to keep Jon steady—he's more thrown by this dreadful business than he lets on. What had the police to say?'

Kate told her of the grass shears theory.

'I'd better go out to the toolshed and get rid of ours,' said Stella, smiling, 'unless Jon's already done so.'

'Don't worry, dear. Nobody's on that tack any more.'

She found Henry in a deckchair in the garden, still checking carefully in Bell's rose books.

'I'm fairly sure I've narrowed it down to one of two possibilities. Both of them were pollinated 2 years ago, so that's about right. Neither has a name—not in the books, anyhow. There are six plants of each, and both sets are growing in the paddock at the back of Howth Lodge. Give me another half-hour to check over these last few references to Baby Faurax, to make sure there isn't a third possibility. Then we can go to look.'

'I'll make coffee,' said Kate, returning to the house.

By the time she took the coffee tray out into the garden, Henry had closed the books. 'Nothing more. If Sir Gerald's right about the pedigree, it must be one of those two groups. The codes are SD 4/6 and MA 6/6. Both those positions are in the paddock.'

She gave him his coffee. 'Are we quite clear what we are looking for?'

'One of two things, I think,' said Henry slowly. 'If all 12 plants are there, the blue-rose motive begins to look unpromising. It would help, of course, if one of the plants were actually in bloom, and we could check it as blue. To find all the plants there doesn't completely exclude the motive. Assuming it was an expert who knew what he was after, he might risk leaving them until the hubbub had died down. But I don't really see it like that, do you? It sounds as though that blow was given in the heat of a quarrel. If it were premeditated, the murderer wouldn't have relied on there being some sort of weapon lying about handy for the job.'

Kate told him about the grass shears.

'That makes a sudden quarrel even more probable. If you're setting out deliberately to kill a man, you don't choose an awkward method like that. Either you happen to have the shears with you—in the pocket of your gardening jacket, say—and you whip them out in a rage and strike at Bell's neck. Or they're his own grass shears that are lying on the bench, and ditto.'

'Not his own,' reasoned Kate. 'There's no point in switching to the grafting knife unless the shears—or whatever—belonged to the murderer, and might identify him.'

'Granted. It has to be the pocket of the gardening jacket. And it looks more and more like Wisbech to me. Not the rubbish about his wife being on drugs, but a simple quarrel with Bell because Wisbech thought he was cheating him out of his share in the proceeds of the rose.'

'What's the second thing?' asked Kate. 'You said we were looking for one of two things.'

'Ah yes. The second thing is that the plants have been

taken away. If they have, then we can be pretty sure that Bell was killed because of the rose—and my money goes heavily on a quarrel with Wisbech. Come on, let's go and look. We have to go in the back way. When we've seen what has happened to the rose plants, we'll get the key from the old charwoman and put the books back.'

They followed the directions Dereck Andrews had given them. The wooden fence was not far along the cart track. Since the gate was locked, Henry moved along until he found the place where the barbed wire on top had been snipped through and stripped away for a distance of a yard or so. Beneath it was an old box the reporters must have used to scramble over. He hoisted himself to the fence top, lowered himself on to a box left on the inner side, and turned back to receive the pedigree books from Kate, then to help her over. 'Damn skirt,' she grumbled. She had made a rip in it, catching it on a nail.

Henry was consulting the books, checking on the coded labels on the rows of bushes and stuck into the soil.

'Here's the first group, darling. Group S. Now then, Row D. Here's the row. Position 4. There are 6 plants in Position 4.'

They stood looking at them. The plants did not look all that strong. Two of them bore blooms.

'Would you call that blue?' asked Kate doubtfully.

Henry shook his head. 'Not blue in the sense that Sir Gerald's rose is. More lilac-coloured, or pale mauve. I've seen roses in quite ordinary gardens that look as blue as that. If that's the rose in question, I reckon we can erase it as a motive.'

'Where's the other position?'

He was already studying the labels again, moving along the grass paths—starting to grow unkempt—between the magnificent beds of rose bushes blazing with colour. 'Group M. Here it is. Row A. Position 6. Kate, come over here.'

He was gazing at the row. The soil had been turned over, and not all that long ago. It had dried on top, but still bore traces of freshness. The position was denuded of bushes. 'That settles it,' said Henry.

'Does it?' she pondered. 'Bit cool, isn't it? You have a violent quarrel with Bell, stab him in the neck, then leave him bleeding to death in the greenhouse and go out and dig up his roses.' She glanced instinctively towards the wall where the greenhouse stood, then looked away again. 'And, Henry, I thought you couldn't shift roses at this time of year.'

'These are all in pots, so you can. All right, it's a bit too cold-blooded (though I can just imagine Wisbech doing it, he's got that saturnine sort of face). But suppose whoever it was had lifted the roses already, and Bell caught him at it. They quarrel, the murderer strikes out . . .'

'They have to move to the greenhouse first. The blow was struck there—that's definite, Kippis says.'

'Suppose Bell himself had lifted the roses. And Wisbech comes along and catches him at it. They quarrel in the greenhouse, Wisbech strikes out, etc. Then he picks up the 6 pots of roses, puts them in his car, and off.'

'He wasn't seen by Nellie to come to the cottage.'

'He could have come in by the gate in the back fence.'

Kate nodded agreement. 'That's most likely. But why should Bell have lifted his own roses anyhow?'

'He might have been going to substitute others, to defraud his partner—pretend they were the blues, and, when they came into flower, they weren't blue enough. And he has the real blues growing somewhere else. Or he might just have been going to transfer them to a nursery for propagation, getting ready to commercialise them.'

'It would have to be Clifford's nursery. We can easily check on that by asking him.'

'Sure we can. But let's put the books back in the cottage first. In the very near future, Kate, you've simply got to tell all this to the police.'

'Not until I've got away with one story. I'll tell them tomorrow morning.'

'I don't like it. You could find yourself in a lot of trouble unless you come clean to Wake or Kippis. Wake doesn't like newspaper people anyway. So if he finds one keeping back important information . . .'

'All right. I'll go to him late tonight, when I've sent my piece, and Sam Kippis won't be likely to slip any of it to the others.'

They went back over the fence. 'Damn skirt!' cried Kate angrily. She had ripped it again.

Henry drove to Bridge Cottages. Mrs Lovell came to the door. 'The key's already out.'

'One of the other reporters borrowed it?'

'No. Mrs Clifford—Sally Clifford.'

Henry stared at her. 'Mrs Clifford? You mean the nurseryman's wife?'

'That's it. She borrowed the key half an hour since. She's lost one earring, and thinks it might have dropped off in Mr Bell's house, that night she went there to a party, when he was found dead. She'll be back with the key soon.'

Henry slipped the old woman a couple of pounds. The look of greedy disappointment lessened in her eyes.

'We'll go and knock on the door,' he said. 'Mrs Clifford will let us in. We only want to put back some books we borrowed.'

As they drove past Mrs Cordoni's cottage, Kate waved cheerfully to the window curtains behind which Nellie was certainly posted. 'What a week the old girl must be having!'

Henry led the way to the door of Howth Lodge. He knocked. Silence. 'Mrs Clifford,' he called. 'Mrs Clifford, would you please let us in?'

They waited. Still no sound. Henry stepped back to look at the windows. The curtains were all closed. 'I don't think she can be here.'

'Perhaps she took the key back by some other route.'

'Maybe.' He tried the door handle. The door opened. He stepped inside, calling, 'Mrs Clifford. Mrs . . .' He broke off in astonishment. 'What the devil . . .?' By his side, Kate gasped.

The entrance hall was in chaos. The books had been tumbled from the shelves, the shelves themselves pulled away from the wall, some of the plaster knocked off. A couple of floorboards had been ripped up.

'Someone's gone mad,' whispered Kate.

Henry put out his arm to stop her. He stepped across the littered floor and opened the door to the living-room.

'Good God!' he cried, aghast.

Like the entrance hall, the living-room had been wrecked. On the floor, in the middle of the mess, a woman lay inert, face down. Henry crouched beside her, gently raised one shoulder, then let go with a mutter of horror. One side of her forehead had been crushed by a heavy blow. Mixed in the blood on the rug lay small pieces of yellowish matter from the brain.

He stood up quickly and caught hold of Kate, thinking she might faint. He turned her quickly out of the room, righted a chair in the hall and sat her in it. 'Put your head down, darling.'

'I'm all right,' muttered Kate weakly. 'Sally Clifford?'

As he nodded, Henry stiffened, listening. 'Stay where you are,' he whispered. 'Don't move.'

He sped across the hall to a door at the end of a small branching corridor. It led to the kitchen, which had also been wrecked. The back door was open to the garden. Through it, he thought he could see something move—a quick movement. Somebody there? He ran to the door. The garden was empty.

He turned slowly back into the kitchen. One of its window-panes, he now noticed, had been smashed so that the window could be unfastened from outside. That, obviously, was how the man got in.

He thought he heard a noise in the garden, turned and ran outside again. Nobody there. But some bushes over by the wall were swaying. Was it only the wind? He went across. One of the boughs of a lilac hung down, recently broken. There were marks on the soil. A man had been there that day, but whether coming or going, or both, Henry could not decide.

He hoisted himself to see over the wall. On the far side was a narrow lane, with woods beyond. No sign of anybody. Henry dropped back into the garden.

The essential was to get the police there quickly. The phone in the cottage—with any luck it had not been cut off. He hastened back through the kitchen into the hall.

The chair in which he had left Kate was empty.

'Kate,' he called. 'Kate, where are you?'

Silence.

The front door was open. Of course, she had gone out to the car. He hurried after her. But there was nobody in the car.

Henry ran back into the house, calling her. He looked into the living-room. The woman's body lay there, as before. But no Kate.

'Kate,' he cried in alarm. 'Kate, where are you?'

He raced upstairs. She lay on the floor of the big bedroom. Her handbag, which had fallen before her, had burst open and scattered its contents across the carpet.

CHAPTER VIII

THE FIRST THING of which she was aware when she woke was dimmed sunlight filtering through window curtains; then the cleanness of walls. Henry's face appeared above her. 'You're all right, darling,' he soothed her. 'Lie still and sleep. You're all right.'

She relapsed into unconsciousness.

The nurse said: 'The sedation is working, Mr Theobald. It'll be hours before she's properly awake. You'd better take a rest and get some food. There's a canteen on the ground floor.'

He went down to the hospital canteen. The house surgeon who took her in Casualty had assured him she was in no danger—slight concussion, perhaps, but nothing to be unduly perturbed about. The blow on the side of the head had only tangented.

Getting himself a cup of coffee and a thick sandwich, Henry sat at an empty table by the window. It overlooked a small yard in which the ambulances were parked. The canteen was almost empty in mid-afternoon. He sat staring at the pale colour of his coffee, cursing himself over again for having been so stupid as to leave her in that house, even for a few minutes.

His shoulder was touched. Dereck Andrews. 'How is she?'

'Nothing to worry about, thank God. She probably has slight concussion, but the doctor sees nothing serious She's under sedation for the next few hours.'

'Won't she be able to phone a piece to the *Post*?'

'Not a chance. They've been trying to get me on the phone, and that blasted photographer keeps hopping round.'

'She'll be devastated,' said Dereck, 'if her own best story doesn't go exclusive into her own rag. Would you like to tell me what happened, and I'll put it through to the *Post* for her?'

Even in his weariness, Henry looked at him with suspicion. But then he remembered that Andrews couldn't do anything for his own newspaper until the following Sunday. So he told him briefly what had happened. 'Thanks, Dereck,' he said. 'Kate'll be grateful.'

'Glad to help. She's a good girl. Got any idea what it's all about, Henry?'

Henry shook his head. He didn't want to think of it. Already he had been through it exhaustively with Inspector Kippis. Now it seemed he was to go through it again. For Kippis was entering the hospital canteen, looking for him, followed by the tall figure of Roger Wake himself. Wake sat at the table. Kippis fetched coffee from the serving counter.

'I hear that Mrs Theobald is not badly hurt,' Wake began. 'That's good news indeed. I shall want to see her, of course, as soon as possible.'

'She's under sedation.'

'When she's fit to talk. The risk you both took was foolhardy. I warned her not to try to follow up on her own matters which she did not fully understand. I don't know whether she told you.'

'Yes,' muttered Henry unhappily, 'she told me.'

'Then how you, Mr Theobald, as a member of the Bar . . .'

'I reproach myself very much. But at the time it seemed a quite reasonable thing to do. My wife was convinced that the rose Bell was supposed to have bred might be behind the whole business. When we found that the bushes had actually been moved, it seemed a bit odd. Come to that, it still does.'

'Didn't it occur to you that they might have been

moved in the ordinary course of Mr Bell's gardening
activities?'

'I suppose so,' admitted Henry weakly. 'But, anyway,
we had to return the pedigree books, and all the newspaper people had been visiting the cottage with the charwoman's key. So the thought of any risk never entered
my mind. By hindsight, of course, it was ridiculous.'

'I want to warn you, Mr Theobald, that there could
be a great deal of risk in this whole matter. I hope you
will pass on the warning, in the strongest possible terms,
to your wife. Detective-Inspector Kippis has been most
helpful to the press and has given out each day all the
information that could be released. Impress on Mrs
Theobald, please, that he will continue to do so, and that
she would be very ill-advised to try any more amateur
detective work of her own. And you too, Mr Theobald. I hope that is clear.'

'Quite clear, Mr Wake,' said Henry soberly. But his
thoughts were not sober. Once he was sure that Kate
was all right, he would take good care not to expose her
to any more risk. But for himself he made no such mental
promise. The images of the wretched Clifford woman
with her brain spilling at the edge of the rug, and of
Kate's sprawled figure on the bedroom floor, were too
vivid in his mind, no matter what this policeman threatened. He was in it personally now.

A nurse called him 5 hours later. He had fallen asleep
on a couch in the outpatients' waiting-room. 'Your wife's
awake, Mr Theobald. Please don't stay too long or get
her excited.'

'And a fine bodyguard you turned out to be,' complained Kate from the pillow on which her bandaged
head was propped.

'I thought I heard somebody outside,' he explained.
'But by the time I got out through the kitchen, there was

nobody. A window was broken, where I suppose he got in, and the door to the garden was open. I fancied somebody had scrambled over the wall behind some bushes, but it must have been the way he got in. And while I was ferreting about in the garden, he was still in the house, and you . . . Darling, are you all right to tell me what happened?'

He could see that she was still weak, but guessed it would be better if she talked about it.

'I went upstairs,' she began.

'Why did you? It was one hell of a risk.'

'I know that now, sweetie. For heaven's sake don't preach, or I'll burst into hysteria. I wanted to put the letters back into the secret compartment in the dressing chest.'

'You took them away? I've already had one towsing from Detective Chief Superintendent Wake, who is far from pleased with you. When he hears about this . . .'

Ignoring that, Kate said, 'So I went to put them back. I was just crossing the bedroom floor when I heard a noise behind me. I tried to jump round, but I got this crack on the side of the head, and here we are. The man must have been behind the curtains of the bed.'

'Did you see him?'

'Not properly. Just the impression of a shortish man.'

'Then you've really no idea who it was?'

'None.'

He took her hand and held it gently. 'And those letters, dear?'

'That's what has been bothering me. They were in my handbag.'

'Your handbag,' Henry told her, 'was lying open on the floor, with the contents all over the carpet. I shoved everything back without looking. Whether there was still a packet of letters . . .'

He went to the cupboard in the wall. Kate's clothes hung on the rail. Her handbag and shoes were on the shelf above. He opened the handbag, peered inside, and took out a packet of letters in a rubber band.'

Kate expired with relief. 'Whatever the bastard was after, then, it wasn't those letters. But I'm pretty sure they were what Sally Clifford was looking for.'

'They were from Sally Clifford?' he asked in astonishment.

Kate turned her head on the pillow. 'They're a bit embarrassing,' she said in a low voice.

Henry removed the rubber band and began to read. But after a short while he folded the letters again and slipped the band back on. Letters like that were not for anybody but the lover to read.

He reflected wryly how wrong local gossip can be. Sally Clifford, the reserved, shy woman whom Nellie Cordoni had thought not to be on Bell's list, was enmeshed with him more closely than any other could have been. The letters were simple, not elaborate, but they shook with passion. So every day, when she had gone out riding, she had crossed the fields and woods to the back door of his garden, like some latter-day Madame Bovary. In so easy a way had she avoided gossip. Nellie Cordoni surveyed the front of the house, and Bell's secret mistress slipped in through the rose garden at the back. And if his mistress could come that way, so of course could his killer. The list of people seen to enter the front of the house on Friday, Henry at once realized, was meaningless.

Nor was it difficult to perceive who the killer had been. Bovary himself—Jack Clifford, the husband, probably an insensitive man, drinking too much, coarse perhaps, but erupting with rage at the sudden discovery of his wife's infidelity; running and stumbling as he hastened through the fields and the empty woods, confronting Bell in his greenhouse, angrily accusing him; then, in a sudden fury as the man turned his back on him with contempt, grasping the grass shears that happened to be in his jacket pocket and striking them into Bell's throat. He might, pondered Henry, even get away with a plea of guilty to manslaughter.

So it had been Clifford who had broken into Howth Lodge this morning and torn down furniture in his search. Search for what? For the letters, perhaps, lest they incriminate him. Then his wife, herself seeking the letters and not realizing that Clifford was there, had taken the key from the old woman and entered the house, to find her husband raging through it, out of control. And he had struck out at her, smashing the side of her skull in his rage.

'The letters must go to Roger Wake at once,' he said uneasily.

'I know,' mumbled Kate from the pillow. 'Do you think he'll be *very* cross with me?'

'I doubt if he'll want to recommend you for that medal for helping the police.'

'Then he'll be stupid, darling. If it hadn't been for me, he would never have known they exist. The police had already searched the house without knowing about the dressing chest.'

'That's true,' Henry admitted. It was unlikely that they would have found the letters in that delicately-contrived compartment. Certainly Clifford would not have found them by pulling down bookshelves and tearing up floorboards, even if he had not been interrupted by the arrival of Kate and himself.

'I'm going now, Kate. I'll take the letters to the Superintendent straight away. They could be vital. You go back to sleep, and don't worry. I'll give him the line of your skill in finding the letters at all.'

At the door he looked back and chuckled. 'Once, at school, I fed Epsom salts in beef gravy to the headmaster's wife's black poodle. I had to own up, of course. And I got the awful summons to the head's study. I've never felt like that since—until now!'

CHAPTER IX

WHEN HENRY TELEPHONED the hospital next morning, the ward sister said: 'Your wife is up and dressed, Mr Theobald, and says to come and fetch her.'

'But is that all right? Does the doctor say she may?'

'Well . . .'

Kate cut in: 'I'm listening on an extension, darling. What the doctor, who's frightfully good-looking and young, actually said was that a girl thick enough to discharge herself from hospital hasn't got much to fear from a blow on the head.'

'Now, look, Kate, don't be rash.'

'What really cured me, darling, was the *Post* this morning. Have you seen page one? Who sent it? Did you arrange it?'

'Lawks, I completely forgot to tell you.'

'Rat,' she said, but pleasantly.

'It was Dereck, of course. He said if I'd tell him what happened, he'd put a piece through for you. So I did. Was that all right?'

'I thought it would be Dereck. He fancies me, you know. Told me once that, if he didn't like you so much, he'd take me to bed willing. Dereck's very sweet. The pictures weren't bad either. Somebody must have primed Horace.'

'Must have been Dereck. Horace has been pestering me, but on principle I wouldn't tell him anything. Butch has been on the phone, full of glory-be-to-Kate, and tell her to stay in hospital until quite recovered, and her name's been put up to the editor for a bonus—£50, Butch thinks.'

'It'll be in multiples of £2.50. The editor has decimalized his personal unit, which is the only one he can think in, the price of a bottle of gin. I say, that's rather good news, darling. Come and fetch me, and let's quietly celebrate. But first put on the kettle for a strong cup of tea. Detective Chief Superintendent Wake wants to see me, and I've told him I'll be at the Old Rectory at 11. By the way, did he raise hell about the letters?'

'He should have been a headmaster. Okay, I'll be there with the car in half an hour.'

When Roger Wake arrived at the Old Rectory he was more affable than Henry expected. Kate was sitting at a table on the garden terrace. Henry led the policeman out, then went to make the tea.

'What I chiefly want,' said Wake, 'is your account of the attack on you. Your husband says you had some brief glimpse of a man. What exactly do you remember?'

Kate pondered. 'I scarcely saw him at all. The only impression I have is that he was not very tall—and I'm not sure I actually *saw* that. The impression may have come from the blow on my head—the angle of it. I honestly don't know.'

'Why are you sure it was a man?'

'Now you ask, I'm not sure. But I think it was—it must have been.'

'Any sound you remember?'

'Only the sound that made me turn. No, not a footstep. The room's carpeted, anyhow. I think it was just the sound of movement from behind the bed curtains.'

'Smell?'

She hesitated. 'I think there was a sort of scent, now you say it. Brilliantine? Sort of lavender? I don't know.

A vague memory of a hair-oily kind of smell, not all that strong.'

The detective was silent.

'Have you forgiven me about the letters, Mr Wake?' she asked. 'I was going to put them back and tell you about them directly, honest I was. And it wasn't until that awful business yesterday that I realized how important they are. How could I?'

'I've said my say to your husband, Mrs Theobald,' he told her in a voice like a wagging finger. 'I'll not go for you. Invalids get special consideration.'

'And you wouldn't have found the letters at all, would you, if it hadn't been for me? Come on now, be fair.'

'You're an invaluable young lady,' he conceded with a thin smile. 'But I do want you to understand how dangerous it is for an amateur to jump to conclusions. You've assumed from those letters that Mrs Clifford was having an affair with Nicholas Bell, and that her husband found out and, in a rage, killed Bell. Isn't that your assumption?'

'Yes, of course.'

'It's totally wrong—at least, not quite totally. Mrs Clifford was having an affair with Bell, but it ended months ago.'

'How do you know?'

'If you had looked carefully at the letters, in the way a police officer would, you might have noticed that the last one was dated last November.'

'Do you get dates on love letters?'

'You get postmarks on envelopes.'

'Hey, Henry,' she called to her husband, who was emerging with the tea tray, 'come and listen. I'm being put firmly in my place. We were wrong about the letters.'

'Wrong?'

'The affair between Bell and Sally Clifford ended last November. We didn't look at the postmarks.'

'I should have thought, Mr Theobald,' said Wake drily, 'that a legal training . . .'

Henry felt as though he had blushed. 'Now, be fair. I looked at only the first couple, then decided they were maybe police business, but were certainly none of mine.'

'A good decision, Mr Theobald, if a little tardy.' He took the cup of tea from Kate. 'Plenty of sugar in it? Good. Of course, the dates of the letters don't prove that the affair ended months ago. This is confidential information I'm now going to give you. We questioned Mr Clifford. I'm telling you only so that you don't go publishing some wild, imaginary story, and put a spanner in the real work—my work, Mrs Theobald.'

'So you questioned Jack Clifford.'

'It was last November that he discovered what was happening. There was thought of a divorce. He even consulted a solicitor. He showed me the solicitor's correspondence—correctly dated last December, Mrs Theobald. But then, for the sake of their daughter, they decided to stay together, and Mrs Clifford gave Bell up.'

'But how could they possibly have gone on with Bell socially?' asked Henry. 'Damn it, when we met them they were in his house for drinks.'

'To cover up, avoid scandal, and keep everything from their daughter. Bell didn't know that Clifford had found out. By agreement with her husband, Mrs Clifford broke with Bell on some story that she feared the daughter was noticing things. I don't suppose he was particularly reluctant to end it. He had other women, and never kept any for long. But it told on Mr Clifford. You've probably heard in the village that lately he has been drinking too much.'

'The rose business not doing well, they said.'

'Maybe not. But the real reason, I take it, was the domestic one. So, you see, there was no sudden discovery by a husband who rushes off in a rage and stabs the lover. The crime of passion you have been picturing did not exist.'

'Then why,' demanded Kate, 'did Mrs Clifford go to the cottage yesterday to try to recover her letters?'

'Assuming that was her purpose—and I think it may have been—it seems natural that she should have wanted to get them back and destroy them. The cottage was being subjected to police searches, and would later presumably be sold, and the contents dispersed. If they had been your letters, Mrs Theobald, wouldn't you have tried to get them back?'

'All right,' agreed Henry. 'So the homicidal maniac loose in this village isn't Jack Clifford, and it wasn't he who was tearing the cottage to bits yesterday. Do you yet know who it is? And what he was looking for? Off the record.'

'We are following certain lines of enquiry . . .'

'During which time a woman has been battered to death, and another, who happens to be my wife, nearly killed.'

'Any information it's in the public interest to disclose,' replied Wake stiffly, rising, 'will be given to the newspaper reporters by Inspector Kippis.'

'You narked him badly, Henry,' she said when Wake had gone. 'Was that wise?'

'Suppose not. But he talks as though he were investigating a minor case of fraud. And you might have been killed.'

'So what was the man looking for?' she softly asked, as though asking herself.

'The only thing worth taking that I saw,' said Henry, 'was the case of brandy in the bottom of the dining-room cupboard.'

'He pulled down bookshelves and ripped some of the wall plaster.'

'The plaster probably came away when he wrenched out the shelves.'

'He pulled up floorboards, tipped everything out of cupboards or drawers . . . He must have been looking for something that he expected to be very well hidden. I say . . .' She was reaching for her handbag, looking speculative. 'What we have overlooked, Henry, is that the letters were not the only things in that chest.' Fumbling with her fingers, she drew out a worn envelope from which she took the faded newspaper clipping. 'We forgot this. We even forgot,' she murmured happily, 'to tell the Superintendent about it.'

He read it over her shoulder. It was a report of a court martial at Kuala Lumpur 15 years ago, of a Captain Stallwood who was charged with cowardice in the face of the enemy. 'What happened to the poor devil?' he asked, turning the clipping over. 'Medical evidence. Discharged. Recommended to be returned to the United Kingdom for psychiatric treatment. So what?'

'Malaya,' Kate pondered. 'That's the only link. Colonel Barrington was killed in Malaya.'

'Colonel Barrington?'

'The alcoholic widow's dear departed. I wonder whether Major Sykes served in Malaya too.'

'Major Sykes?'

'Don't keep on parroting names, there's a dear boy. Wilfred Sykes, who's in love with Mamie Barrington, according to your favourite newscaster, Nellie Cordoni.'

Stella Sims came out from the house. 'You're wanted on the phone, Kate. It's your office. Man with a lovely growl in his voice wants to know if you're well enough to talk to him.'

'That'd be Butch,' said Kate, going in. 'Hallo, Butch sweetie.'

'Kate, are you all right? The editor was so upset when

he heard about you that he had to go out for a drink. Matter of fact, he's not back yet. Are you all right?'

'I'm fine. No harm done.'

'It's a great relief. Are you fit enough to come to London? The editor just phoned in, from some club in Soho, to ask if you can get to the afternoon conference. He wants to go into the whole story thoroughly. He says we've got such a lead on all the others that we've simply got to stay ahead now. And he doesn't trust any of us except you.'

'He really is the nicest man.'

'Perhaps Henry could drive you up. Or we could send a car and driver.'

'Nonsense. Henry can put me on the train. I'll stay in our flat for the night, and you can buy me a dinner.'

'Willingly, girl, willingly.'

Henry, when told, wasn't too keen on letting her go alone. But she argued that he could help best by staying in Ashworth and making some quiet enquiries for her. 'Major Sykes and Mamie, darling. And perhaps a side-long glance at Mr Tooth the publican. As Fred put it, we've got to have *somebody* to suspect.'

'What do you want to know?'

'I don't even know that. Just anything you can turn up, using that clever legal brain of yours.'

As he put her on the train, he begged her to be careful and not to overdo things. She promised to be in bed by 10 and to ring him from the flat to reassure him.

The train pulled out from Linchester station. She unfolded the *Post* to read the front page over again, smiling pleasantly. A face appeared over the newspaper.

'Oh, Horace, it's you.'

'You might have told me you were going up to the office.'

'Since you already know,' she replied wearily, 'there was no need.'

'I got a tip-off from the art desk, or I wouldn't have known. Why can't we co-operate? And do you always travel second? I'm in a first, next carriage along the train, nearer the buffet.'

'Don't let me keep you from it.'

'No, I'll stay with you,' he decided, sitting opposite her. 'We ought to discuss the story.'

Which, Kate suddenly told herself, wasn't a bad idea. 'Why not? It's time you did some work on it, Horace. Now, don't get ratty—I'm only pulling your leg. There is something, but I don't know that it's possible, even for the best picture-snatcher in the business.'

'Try me.'

She took the clipping from the envelope in her handbag and passed it to him. 'Do you think there's any chance of getting a picture of Captain Stallwood?'

Horace noted the details of the clipping on the back of his packet of cigarettes; a habit which Kate had often observed in newspaper photographers. 'Leave it to Horace, sister.'

'I'll buy you a cup of tea,' she volunteered.

He led the way to the buffet car, complaining to the barman of the swaying of the train. 'Bloody railways charge twice as much as anybody else for a cup of tea, and half of it slops into the saucer because they don't maintain their track properly. You ought to take a lesson from the French railways. They run their trains properly.'

'Ah,' agreed the barman. 'But they make lousy cups of tea.'

Kate said, 'Horace, you stay here and drink your tea. I'm going back to the compartment. I've got some hard reading to do. See you at the terminus.'

She made her way back along the corridor, entering a compartment in which only one man was seated at the far corner. She had seen him on her way to the buffet.

'Good morning, Dr Wisbech,' she said brightly.

Ignoring his grunt, she settled opposite him to chatter. On the level of bare civility he had to make some sort of answers. Yes, he was going to London for the summer show of the Royal National Rose Society. No, he was not exhibiting. He grew only a few ordinary roses in his garden at Linchester—nothing to dream of showing.

'How about the new roses you've been breeding with poor Mr Bell. Did he intend to exhibit any of them?'

Dr Wisbech really couldn't say.

Kate decided to plunge. 'I've heard there was one very interesting new rose that Mr Bell was going to call after Stella Sims. A cross, I think, between one of the seedlings you and Mr Bell raised, and Baby Faurax.'

The man was staring at her. Then he grunted that he had no knowledge of what Bell intended to name any rose.

Kate said, 'The 6 plants have been dug up from the position where Mr Bell planted them in his paddock.'

'What position? How could you possibly know any of Bell's planting positions? They're all coded.'

'Oh,' Kate murmured with deliberate vagueness, 'on murder cases the press and the police always work closely together.'

She had expected a momentary panic in his eyes, but he continued to stare coldly at her, unmoved.

'Have you any idea,' she asked, 'whether it was Mr Bell himself who moved those roses, or could it have been someone else? And, if so, who?'

'I know nothing whatever about roses being moved. Bell often shifted his roses about. As for the blue one, I've no idea what happened to it, if anything.' He opened a thin briefcase lying on the seat beside him, extracting a printed set of lectures. 'And now Mrs Theobald, you must excuse me. I have work on which I must concentrate.'

'So sorry,' she murmured sweetly. 'I'll go back to my own carriage, not to disturb you.'

She went smiling to herself. That had been a bad slip—when he spoke of the blue rose.

CHAPTER X

SHE WAS RECEIVED gladly at the office. Butch patted her bottom approvingly and told her the editor was back and had signed the chit for her bonus.

'Buy you all a drink,' she offered. So several went round to the Press Club for half-an-hour's amiable conversation and a number of large gins.

'What's the truth, Kate?' asked Butch. 'Is it this rose-grower that did both Bell and his own wife? What's his name? Clifford.'

'No, neither. I had it from Roger Wake himself, this morning, as guidance. He was afraid I might go hinting just that. According to him, Jack Clifford's in the clear.'

'Perhaps he's just trying to head us off,' suggested one of the others.

Butch who had once been a crime reporter, shook his head. 'I knew Wake quite well a few years back. He hates newspapermen—or, rather, reckons they're a nuisance. So he keeps what he can from us. But he wouldn't deliberately mislead.'

Kate confirmed that. When she had challenged him with trying to make use of her, he had at once admitted it.

'Curious chap,' Butch mused. 'I once thought he must be a queer. But I don't think he is. More like a sort of recluse, or a scholar. I once came across him in a pub drinking lemonade. He's a teetotal non-smoker, as you know, without any interest in women. Collects stamps, maybe. Anyway, there he was, reading Yeats. You'd think he was educated, which in a policeman is absurd. Come on, back to the office.'

Kate wandered into the clippings library. Luckily Reggie, the library boy, her friend and stalwart, was on duty. Would a court martial of a British officer in Malaya 15 years ago have been reported over here? The charge was cowardice.

'Sure to have been,' nodded Reggie, taking the name and date, climbing to the top of the long rows of dusty steel shelves, pulling out a thick folder, shaking the dirt off it and flipping through the hundreds of clippings it contained, pasted up on sheets of paper. 'Here you are, Mrs Theobald.'

She sat at an obscure desk behind the shelves to read it. But it wasn't as full as the clipping she already had from the *Straits Times*. And there was no background stuff, no follow-up. There wouldn't have been. A British officer charged with cowardice was not a case the London newspapers would spread themselves on. It had to be reported, of course, but left at that. She asked Reggie if there were any more on Captain Stallwood himself, straight out under his own name. But there wasn't. She sat staring at the one clipping, reading it again, but it conveyed nothing further to her.

Reggie called across the room, 'Horace on the blower for you, Mrs Theobald!'

'I've got the picture you wanted,' came Horace's voice.

'Nice work.' She was genuinely impressed.

'And there's something else too. Can you come and look?'

'Come where?'

'It's a small picture agency that specializes in Far East stuff.' He gave her an address in one of the courtyards leading off Fleet Street.

It was at the very top of a steep staircase so old and uneven that she tripped once on the way up; on the dirty frosted glass of the door, in letters half worn away: 'Far East Pictures Ltd. Prop. E. Tong.'

The room was stacked with metal filing cabinets, on top of which were piled hundreds of assorted cardboard files, crammed with old and cracked prints, in no apparent sort of order. A little light filtered through a skylight that could not have been cleaned for years, perhaps decades. It was dimly reinforced by a few naked electric bulbs suspended among the cabinets. She wandered uncertainly in, then discovered, round a bluff of cabinets, a small desk with Horace sitting on it and a thin, elderly, snuffling man in a torn woollen cardigan behind it, with the remains of a hand-rolled cigarette twisted into his lips. Mr Tong, introduced Horace. He didn't look Chinese, but perhaps had lived in Stepney for a long time, or perhaps he was native; Tong, after all, is a possible English name.

Horace handed her a close-up print of a man of about 30, in uniform, three pips on his shoulder. On the back was scribbled, 'Captain Hugh Y. Stallwood. See Straits Times.' And it gave the date and page reference.

'It won't print,' Horace told her. 'Mr Tong rephotographed a half-column half-tone in that issue and blew it up. We could photograph the repro. and have a go, but by the time you got it on newsprint it could be anybody.'

'Doesn't matter,' said Kate. Even as it was, to make out details of the face was not easy. He was evidently a handsome, conventional Army officer. But the high forehead and the weak line of the mouth suggested, she told herself, an introspective, unhappy nature. What he had to do, if anything, with the business at Ashworth, she had no idea. 'What was the other thing, Horace?' she asked.

He hauled a heavy, stained, tattered file of newspapers on to the desk. 'Straits Times for that year,' he informed her. 'Mr Tong has a wonderful collection, covers most

of the Far East wherever there were newspapers in
English or French, and goes back before 1914.' He looked
admiringly at Mr Tong, who showed no appreciation,
but held a match to the charred fragment in his lips. Only
by long practice, Kate thought, could it be possible
to do so without evaporating the permanent dewdrop at
the end of his nose.

'So we turned up the date of your clipping,' Horace
was telling her, 'then worked back to when the story
broke. There wasn't much about it.'

'Perhaps we had a censorship going, while the fighting
was still on.'

'Don't know,' said Horace. 'Shouldn't think so. Bloody
Army isn't fly enough, and the bloody politicians create.
Anyway, while we were going back through the issues,
Mr Tong and me, we ran across this. What d'you think?'

He swivelled the file so that Kate could see a 2-column
block of a man in a light gabardine suit against a background of palm trees, with tall white office buildings in
the distance. The man had a cigarette in his fingers and
was smiling knowingly. Kate stared at the picture for
a minute, then suddenly grasped what Horace meant.

'Nicholas Bell?' she asked.

'Could be,' he said. He pulled from his pocket the
blow-up of the picnic snapshot that Stella Sims had pro-
vided, and laid it by the side of the newspaper block,
face beside face.

'It's certainly very like,' Kate admitted. Anybody who
had known Bell in life could have told at once whether
or not it was he, she thought, even allowing for the 15
years' difference in age. 'But doesn't the story say?'

'Different name,' replied Horace.

She began to read. It was one of those investigations
which newspapers love to conduct into what promised
to be a financial scandal. The man principally involved
—the man in the picture with the palm trees—was named

as Thomas Stevens, a businessman with an address in Singapore. Kate could not take in the details of the alleged scandal. It was something to do with buying up copra plantations and floating companies to develop them.

'Did anything come of it?'

'Can't find anything,' said Horace. 'We've looked through the files for quite a long way ahead, and there's nothing. And Mr Tong doesn't remember any big case.' He glanced admiringly again at the little old man behind the desk. 'Wonderful memory, Mr Tong. Never knew anyone like it. Only for the Far East, though—eh, Mr Tong?' Mr Tong slightly nodded assent. To Kate's fascination, the nod wobbled the dewdrop but did not dislodge it. It held.

'I'll get Reggie on it in the library,' she said. 'I've got to get back to the office for the afternoon conference.'

Reggie said he'd do his best, but he wasn't hopeful, the name was too usual. He came down his ladder with 3 files which he set on the desk before her.

Two she could reject quickly. One was a politician and the other a priest. The third folder was 'Stevens—General.' She moved through the initials to 'T', reflecting uneasily that Thomas might easily have been a second name, so that she'd miss him if he were, for example, William T. Stevens. However, she'd try the Thomases first.

There were only a dozen. Five she could reject because they were dead, 3 more because in the year in question they were doing things that ruled them out as possible businessmen in Malaya.

She turned to the last 4. The first was an actor, but when she came across the date of his birth she realized he was much too old. The second was an athlete who had married a girl in Brixham, and had been interviewed there, where he kept a sports shop, in the last Olympics year. Kate noted him for a quick enquiry at Brixham. He wasn't likely. The third had been fined quite recently for taking violent part in a student demonstration. There were no dates, but clearly he was too young. The only remaining clippings were of a Thomas Stevens who had been sentenced to 2 years for armed robbery, 18 years ago. The robbery had been in London at Stoke Newington. And there was a clipping from a local weekly, after the trial. There weren't many such in the library, which concentrated on nationals. Perhaps the then librarian lived at Stoke Newington. And it carried a picture of Thomas Stevens.

Kate stared at it. The man was much younger, of course—in his early twenties.

She could not be sure. She wished like hell she had seen Bell himself, just once, when he was alive.

'Hey, Reggie,' she called suddenly, 'get the darkroom to do me a blow-up of that one, will you? I'd like several copies. See if you can get them quickly enough to send into the conference.'

As she walked through the big office, she grew more and more convinced. She'd have to check it through the police. She grinned to herself at the thought of casually putting it to Roger Wake. But somehow, now she knew —or almost knew—that Nicholas Bell had been a criminal. And the whole thing looked, from that angle, absolutely different.

Nobody could have told, when the editor came in to take the conference, that he had been on the gin for 24 hours. He was such a tall, thin, spruce, dapper man. The only indications even faintly suspicious were a slight flush round the nostrils, and the pink gleam of his forehead where it merged with the baldness of his skull. He greeted Kate with a word of praise, but did not shake hands with her. The editor disliked shaking hands, or any other contact with a fellow human. His distaste for the race, it was sometimes said, was the core of his success as a political editor.

They took the politics first, the editor and the Lobby man engaging in a quiet, technical duologue that might have been in code for all Kate grasped of it. That settled the subject of the leader, which the editor would write himself, as he always did, no matter how thick the alcoholic haze. The features editor came in next with the usual trite, whimsy topics; then dear Clara, smiling through her thick spectacles, roughed out the proposed contents of the women's pages. The financial editor interpolated a brief talk on the expected import-export figures for the month. Nobody bothered to talk to the sports editor, who sat silent through every conference and filled his pages without discussion with anybody—certainly not with the editor, since they loathed each other. The foreign editor synopsized the latest developments in the crisis in the Middle and Far Easts. The art editor flushed the long table with stacks of newly-fixed, damp prints, drawing particular attention to the outsize nipples on a profile of a minor actress's breasts. The news editor ran down his list of strikes, riots, drug prosecutions, sexual deviations, conflagrations, deaths, disputes, interviews on the state of society with show-business celebrities, and all the other normal incidents of the day's life in the home islands.

'And now,' said the editor, who had listened to it all with compulsive attention, 'the blue rose murders. This is what we're actually selling copies on. I've had a note from Circulation. Yesterday we put on 143,000, and this morning a further 213,000. They've no doubt it's the cumulative effect of the lead we've had on this story. And we're going to stay on it. Butch?'

'It's mostly Kate's pigeon,' he said. 'But we've been doing a bit of work on it this end. The botanist, Dr

Wisbech, who helped Bell breed the blue rose, was in London today for the Rose Show. He wouldn't talk, but we've got a bit about him from another rosarian, and quite a splurge about the rose industry generally.'

'What did you find out about Wisbech?' asked Kate.

'Nothing exciting. I'll let you have a copy of the notes. He led one or two plant-gathering expeditions, years ago, in South America, and there was quite a bit about him getting lost for a couple of weeks in the Matto Grosso. But he turned up safe. He married a woman who'd written a couple of lesbian novels that caused a fuss at the time, though nobody would so much as notice them these days.'

'Nellie Cordoni says she's on drugs, and Bell was the supplier,' put in Kate.

'Could be. Sweet Nellie seems to be reasonably well informed. She was right about the Clifford daughter. She was in trouble with the boys. We traced her to an aunt in Wimbledon, and she's just gone into an abortion clinic in Paddington. Until that cropped up, we thought you might like to do a touching interview with her. But now, of course, it's no go. The only other thing is that Horace has turned up a picture of a man called Thomas Stevens, who was involved in some sort of property scandal in Malaya 15 years ago, which doesn't seem to have come to anything. Horace thinks it's Bell.'

He gestured to the art editor, who proffered several prints that were handed round. 'And here's the one we had of Bell,' said the art editor, passing out another sheaf.

All round the table they stared at the two prints side by side.

'Well, Kate?' asked the editor.

'I'm not sure. There's no denying the resemblance, and there is some sort of curious link with Malaya—oh, nothing specific, but it crops up once or twice about people in the village. I wish I'd seen Bell himself.'

'You did.'

She shuddered. 'Not to recognize.'

'The resemblance isn't all that marked,' said the foreign editor.

'Remember there's 15 years' difference,' Kate reminded them. 'And, if Nicholas Bell and Tom Stevens are the same person, then there's another possibility. I went through the Stevens folder in the library. There's one Tom Stevens who went down for 2 years for robbery with violence, about 18 years ago. And there's a picture of him. He was in his early twenties then—if it was Bell. I've asked for some blow-ups to be sent in. Ah, here they come.'

The boy from the darkroom dropped a pile of damp prints before Kate. She passed one to the editor, one to Butch, and dealt the rest round the table.

For a long minute they all stared in silence at the sets of 3 photographs. Then Butch declared, 'Too damn risky.'

'We can't libel Bell,' murmured Kate. 'He's dead.'

'But you could libel Thomas Stevens,' put in the lawyer from his seat beside the editor, 'if so be he isn't Nicholas Bell after all.'

The news editor was buzzing through to his desk. 'Got the P.A. tape yet of this afternoon's press conference at Linchester? Good. Send it in.'

He took the teleprinted slips from the boy who brought them, and began to read : 'Became known this afternoon that Nicholas Bell, the rose hybridist, who was found murdered in his garden greenhouse last Friday, had a criminal record. Detective Chief Superintendent Roger Wake, in charge of the case, had his fingerprints sent to Scotland Yard as a matter of routine, a police spokesman said, and they disclosed his real identity. Under another name, he had served a prison sentence, some years ago, for robbery with violence. Police withholding Bell's real name for the time being, while they pursue their enquiries.'

The editor glanced swiftly round, then snapped out his decision : 'That settles it. We disclose the name tomorrow.'

'Should we check with the Yard first?' asked the news editor.

'No. All you'd get would be a dusty answer. We have to take the risk. Kate, you write it.'

'Do we link Tom Stevens the armed robber with Tom Stevens in Malaya?' she queried. 'Or do we just stick with the robbery in Stoke Newington?'

The editor turned to the lawyer. 'If we're wrong on one or both counts, how much'll it cost?'

The lawyer pondered. 'If you're wrong about the man sentenced for robbery, and he goes for us, he wouldn't get all that much. Say £7,000. We'd have to settle, of course. Costs could be astronomic. If it is the Malayan gent you're wrong about, and he isn't the same as the young robber, it could cost plenty.'

'£25,000?'

'Should cover it.'

'Then go ahead,' said the editor. 'Bill, get all you can about the Stoke Newington robbery, but stay away from police sources. Geoffrey, start the stringer in Kuala Lumpur digging out all he can about the property scandal, and Thomas Stevens. Don't tell him what it's for, or link it with Bell in any way.'

'It's about 1 a.m. tomorrow morning in Malaysia,' said the foreign editor. 'The poor devil will be in bed.'

'Then get him out of bed,' instructed the editor, rising abruptly to seek his own room where he could write his political leader.

She sat thumping out the piece on a typewriter in the

big room. Butch hovered, taking the copy sheet by sheet. At the last one he kissed her. 'Good girl. You've earned your dinner.'

'Not just the two of us, Butch. Think what your reputation would do to mine. Henry would hit you in the eye.'

He laughed. 'As though you weren't a match for any six men! But still your maiden fears. Bill and Geoffrey are both coming, and Clara, and Bill's old woman, and Geoffrey's fancy bit. Bill's booked a table at some joint in Soho where he says his credit's good. And we thought we'd start at one or two of the familiar hostelries.'

'I'll just go and clean up,' said Kate, 'and send the boy out for a tube of Alka-Seltzer. And I want a solemn oath that you'll all deliver me in one piece, before midnight, to our flat in Chelsea.'

'Done,' agreed Butch.

They started decorously with champagne at El Vinos, and moved up to the Old Cock for a chaser. After that Kate lost track of pub names. There was one somewhere behind the Law Courts, and a snug little bar just off Long Acre. Mostly they drank either beer or scotch. Geoffrey's fancy bit, name of Freda, who had unwisely opted for gin-and-mixed, began to laugh so loudly at Butch's jokes that she had to be quietened with a nice long lager beer. Clara, whose Fleet Street experience was lengthy, was lasting with considerable dignity. Bill's wife, who Kate decided was a dear, drank chiefly sherry. They had a quick refresher of champagne by the glass in Maiden Lane and drifted into the Salisbury for their last scotch before dinner. They arrived at the restaurant in two taxis and reasonable order, except for Freda's insistence on leaving the taxi on all fours. Then the food, which was delicious, helped. So far as Kate could make out, they had a Pouilly Fumé with the fish, some sort of very tasty claret with the tournedos Rossini, and skipped

the rest to choose from port, brandy or Cointreau with
the coffee. Kate had a Drambuie with hers. It was as
well that the restaurant was by now nearly empty, for
they were kicking up a fair amount of noise, and at one
point Butch insisted on making a speech, stopping half-
way with the admission that he couldn't think of a damn
thing to say. The commissionaire got them a couple
of taxis. Geoffrey scooped Freda up from the front steps
and placed her carefully in one, and had then to be dis-
suaded from seating himself in the space beside the driver
reserved for luggage. 'It's the little things, Geoffrey,' said
Butch, gently steering him into the interior, 'that give
you away.'

Outside her small block of flats in Chelsea, Kate care-
fully kissed all the men in turn. So did Freda. Leaving
Geoffrey to cope with her as best he could, Bill and
Butch took Kate up the stairs to her own flat door, helped
her with the key, switched on the light and saw her in.
She suggested a nightcap, but they thought better not.

When they had gone she plucked off her clothes,
brushed her teeth, searched for a nightdress but failed to
find one, so fell naked into bed.

She was not sure what woke her. Perhaps it was that
she was coughing and choking in her sleep. As she
emerged through the concentric rings of haziness into
semi-wakefulness, she realized she was still coughing
and choking, and her eyes were thick and smarting, her
throat gasping, her nostrils curling at the repulsiveness
of the smell. Then she clicked to fully awake. Gas! The
room was filling with gas. She pushed herself out of bed
and, fighting for breath, went lurching groggily towards
the window.

CHAPTER XI

AFTER HE HAD SEEN his wife off in the train from Linchester that morning, Henry Theobald strolled slowly back to the hired car. Kate's instructions were to make some quiet enquiries about Major Sykes and Mamie Barrington, with a sidelong glance at Billy Tooth the publican. He was wondering how to start. The publican seemed easiest, so he drove back to Ashworth and looked in at the Nag's Head. There were 3 or 4 men in the public bar, but the saloon was empty. The moon-faced girl drew him a pint of best bitter which he sipped while picking over the racing columns of *The Times*.

A few minutes later Billy Tooth appeared behind the bar, starting to polish glasses.

'Morning,' said Henry. 'All your newspaper guests seem to have deserted you.'

'They've all gone to Linchester because of something in the *Post* this morning. Oh, that's your missus, ain't it?'

Henry nodded and sipped his beer, glancing casually over the newspaper at the man. He had been good-looking, but he was not tall and he was now becoming fat. The greying of his sandy hair, the lines around a weak mouth, and the shiftiness of his pale eyes all gave him an anxious look, almost furtive. He was in shirt-sleeves and grey flannel slacks; the shirt not fresh and the trousers bagged.

'Got anything for the Royal Hunt Cup at Ascot?' asked Henry.

The mention of horses enlivened the man. He leaned confidently on the bar, looking over Henry's arm at the list of runners. 'I've put a bit on Slipper.'

'Ten to one?'

'Friend of mine at Newmarket slipped me the info. a couple of months ago,' said Tooth, picking up another glass and wiping it nervously. 'They've been holding it back. I reckon this is the race they've been waiting for. Look at the form. Nothing to touch Slipper if it's the right day.'

'Sounds promising. Can you get something on for me? Quid each way, say? My bookie's in London.'

Tooth seemed to retreat, to curl up behind his eyes. 'There's a betting shop in Linchester, if you're going that way. I deal with a firm in Brighton.' He gave a quick look round, like a reflex, nervous, frightened of something.

'Okay,' said Henry. 'I'll look in at the betting shop lunchtime.' He wondered how he could move closer to making a few discreet enquiries, as Kate had instructed. The bold approach, perhaps. 'You read the report, of course, of my wife getting knocked out in Howth Lodge.'

'Very sorry to hear of it, sir. Is she better?'

'Oh yes, she's all right. But she was lucky. The other woman, Mrs Clifford—well, it's not a sight I'll soon forget. She was horribly battered.'

'Nice, quiet woman too. Kept herself to herself. It's broken Jack Clifford up, poor chap.'

'What's it all about, Mr Tooth? You people who live here must have an idea of it.'

The publican raised his hands helplessly. 'Who'd want to go for Sally Clifford? It don't make sense. Nicky Bell, now, there might have been reasons . . .'

'Not a pleasant chap?'

Tooth came round, vituperative. 'He was a bastard. Once he'd got you, he held on. And always mocking, jeering at you.'

'I think,' said Henry casually, 'that Mrs Clifford was killed only because she happened to interrupt something. She got in the way. Whatever he was looking for, the searcher was feverishly anxious to find it. The interior of that cottage was torn to pieces.'

Tooth lit a cigarette nervously. 'You were in there, sir. Were all Bell's things turned over—all his private papers and that?'

'Every damn thing.'

'Would the police have cleared them away by now?'

'I don't know. I haven't been back. But I shouldn't think so. Why should they?' Henry laughed. 'Something of yours in there that you want to get hold of?'

Tooth hesitated, then leaned forward and asked hoarsely, 'Would you help me?'

'Get something out of that cottage? Not a chance. But maybe I could help you in another way. I'm a lawyer. It's surprising how often people worry about things which, if they knew a little law, they wouldn't fear at all. What's in there that you want? Private papers, you said. Would it be cheques—cheques that bounced?'

The man nodded miserably. 'I had to have money. I'd lost a lot to the bookies.'

'Really a lot?'

'Hundreds. I had to have it. The bookies were starting to threaten—and they didn't mean prosecution. It's the razor, or smashing up your pub . . .'

'So Bell helped out?'

'I gave him post-dated cheques. I told him, when they came due, that they wouldn't be met. But he put them through all the same, just to get them back as proof that they'd bounced. Then he held 'em. Said I could pay him whenever he wanted a drink. Oh, it dragged on. I won't bother you with all that. But what happens if the police get those cheques?'

'You mean, would they prosecute you for cheque offences? I shouldn't think so, Mr Tooth. Not without a complaint from whoever they bounced on. And Bell isn't

116

going to complain any more. But if you mean, would they start thinking of them as a possible motive . . .'

'For doing him in?' Tooth laughed suddenly. 'Oh, that don't worry me. I didn't murder him—never even saw him that morning.'

'You were said to be there for some time—longer than it takes to deliver drinks. Were you looking for the cheques, maybe?'

'No. I knew he'd have hidden 'em away where I'd not find 'em.' He hesitated again. Then: 'You really don't think the police'd have me up on cheque charges?' He blew out his cheeks. 'And you're a lawyer, so you'd know. What a relief! It's been a nightmare.'

'But suppose they probe them as motive.'

'That's all right. I'd tell 'em the truth.'

'Which is?'

'I waited to see him, but he wasn't there.'

'What did you want to see him about?'

Tooth glanced at him, suddenly suspicious. 'You cross-examining me?'

Henry laughed. 'It's my trade. I thought that, if I knew what it was, I might be able to give you a bit more advice.'

Tooth stared at him, then leaned forward again over the bar. 'Right you are. I'd raised some money and I was waiting to pay him. Not all I owed, but some. I'd buy the cheques back in instalments. But he wasn't there, so I came away.'

It sounded genuine enough, Henry thought. But he tried one more test. 'All right. So you've still got the money, and you can show it to the police to back your story. Sounds all right to me. But don't put it all on Slipper.'

The sudden fear in the man's eyes was enough. It was just what he had done—on Slipper, or some other horses.

And probably lost most of it. Which was sufficient evidence that he had had the money, and was therefore telling the truth. Henry reckoned that Billy Tooth could be crossed off the suspect list, if indeed he was ever seriously on it. He was too feeble a specimen for actual violence.

He was about to question Tooth again, but the door of the saloon opened and somebody came in behind him.

'Good morning, Major,' said the landlord, gathering his composure quickly. 'The usual?'

Henry turned. 'Ah, good morning,' he said. 'Didn't we meet at Nicholas Bell's house the night it happened? Major Sykes, isn't it?'

Major Sykes inclined his head gravely. 'Yes, we met there.'

He was, thought Henry, a grave man—a dependable man, a good soldier. He stood straight, moved with the ease of a man in good physical condition. The bone structure of his face was square and strong; but the expression sombre. His thick dark hair was starting to whiten, and his clipped moustache to grizzle.

'Join me in a drink?' asked Henry. The landlord was already pushing a pint tankard of beer across the bar.

'Thank you,' said Major Sykes, taking it. After the first swig he asked, without much interest, 'Are you newspaper people going to be here long in Ashworth?'

'Couldn't say. I suppose it depends on what happens. But it's my wife who writes for a newspaper, not me. I'm at the Bar. It's pure chance we were here at all. Jonathan Sims was at college with me, and we came for the weekend.'

Major Sykes remarked that he didn't know Mr Sims very well, but that his daughter, Mary, liked the wife very much, and saw a lot of her. Henry agreed that Stella was a charming girl.

'By the way, Major,' he asked, 'did you by any chance

serve in Malaya during the Communist uprising there?'

He was surprised at the way the other's eyes narrowed and his head went back, almost as though guarding against a blow. 'Yes, I was there. Why do you ask?'

'Oh, I just wondered if you could help us with a little enquiry my wife is trying to clear up. There was a Captain Stallwood who was courtmartialled on a charge of cowardice, and I think was sent home as a psychiatric case. Fifteen years ago. Did you happen to be there at that time?'

'Stallwood? Stallwood? No, I don't recall it. Must have been just before I was posted there. What are you drinking? Bitter? Billy, let's have those again.'

It was obvious that the man was lying. At the mention of the name he had looked hunted, bewildered. It was obvious, too, that he could not leave it there. He had to know what Henry was getting at. Several times, as they talked desultorily, he seemed on the edge of saying something, but hesitated, then closed his lips. As they were finishing their beer, he asked abruptly, 'Are you doing anything for lunch? If not, would you care to come along to my place for bread and cheese? Mary spends her days at the university. She's studying Natural Science. She leaves a snack out for me at lunchtime. If you'd like to join me . . .'

'Most kind. I'd love to.'

The house was a modern villa, not elegant, 100 yards off the village street, down a lane. The furniture was stiff and ordinary, the pictures heavy Victorian oils in gilt frames. There were a few books, military memoirs, a small encyclopaedia, a large atlas, a row of paperback detective stories. The garden at the back was tidy, a stretch of lawn surrounded by shrubs, but otherwise bare. 'Nice to meet somebody in this village who isn't a rosarian,' said Henry.

'I'm no gardener, and Mary doesn't much care for it.

My wife was devoted to it. In our old place we had a most beautiful garden. But here . . .' He saw the query in Henry's look, and added, 'My wife died 7 years ago.'

He was bringing a tray of bread and cheese from the kitchen and opening a quart bottle of pale ale. They settled to it at a small table by the window, still chatting desultorily. Then Sykes pushed the tray aside.

'I realize you know I was lying to you in the pub. You took me by surprise. I was startled that you knew about it. How much do you know?'

'Some,' said Henry carefully.

'Of course I knew Hugh Stallwood. We were subalterns together. We served in the same regiment. I'm godfather to Ralph, and I've done my best to protect Mamie.'

'Mrs Barrington?' asked Henry, nearly giving away that he had not known. But Sykes was too absorbed to catch the slip.

'She changed her name afterwards, of course. It's her maiden name. And we cooked up a Colonel Barrington, killed in Malaya. Nobody was likely to question it in a village. Nobody in fact ever has—except Bell.'

'He knew?'

'He knew of the court martial, and he knew that Mamie is Hugh's wife. Heaven knows how he knew. We never discovered that.'

'You say his wife. Captain Stallwood is still alive?'

'It wasn't cowardice. Hugh was as brave and as honourable a man as I ever knew. He should never have been courtmartialled. In a home command he wouldn't have been. In a desperately tight situation, with the lives of 50 of his men at stake—there was a Communist ambush—it wasn't his courage that snapped. It was his mind. He has been in a top-security mental hospital for 12 years, Mr Theobald. He will never come out of it. That was what that scoundrel was blackmailing her with.'

'Bell?'

Sykes nodded. 'For years. I found out only recently. For years he has been getting money out of her—not large sums. She said he didn't even seem very interested in the money. It was more as if he were torturing her for pleasure.'

'Why didn't she tell him to go to hell? There's no disgrace in such a tragedy.'

'Because of Ralph. She brought him up to believe the Colonel Barrington story. I begged her not to. When he was still a baby, I begged her to tell him the truth, even before she brought him back to England—she was living out there, her family home was there, her father was a Singapore merchant before he died. But she said she could not contemplate the boy growing up knowing that his father was in a madhouse. She said she would tell him when he was 21. But she won't. She no longer has the strength. One day Hugh Stallwood will die in his cell, and the boy will never know. I shall go to bury him. Then I shall ask Mamie to marry me, and she will refuse. She will refuse, Mr Theobald,' he said quietly, 'because she knows that by then she will be a hopeless alcoholic.'

The two of them sat in silence for what seemed a very long time, until Henry dared ask, 'Why are you telling me this?'

'Because you or your wife seem to have got on to it, and it's a question of newspapers. If it got into print, and everything were made public, I daren't face what would happen between Ralph and his mother. Nor, I fear, dare she. I think she would kill herself. I want your word—for yourself and for your wife.'

Henry gazed at him steadily. 'Major Sykes, when you recently found out that Bell was blackmailing Mrs Barrington, did you kill him?'

The soldier gazed as steadily back. 'I did not. I considered doing so, Mr Theobald, but rejected it for the very reason that you now exemplify I'd have gone to gaol for him. I'd have pleaded guilty with a clear conscience. But inevitably all this would have become public. That was why I didn't kill him. It would have meant killing Mamie by indirect means. I give you my word that the facts about Hugh Stallwood, and Bell's blackmail of Mamie, had nothing whatever to do with his murder. I don't know why he was killed, or who killed him. But it was not because of all this. Now, have I your word?'

'As for my word, it's irrelevant. I'm not a newspaperman. And I have to tell you that there's something that neither my wife nor I can stop, and she may not be willing to, in any event. The reason she knows anything at all about Captain Stallwood is that she found in Howth Lodge an old clipping from the *Straits Times* reporting the court martial. That, presumably, is how Bell knew.'

'How did he associate it with Mamie?'

'That I have no idea.'

'Has your wife given that clipping to the police?'

'Not yet. But I think she must.'

'But why? It has nothing to do with the murder. You have my word on that. To disclose it will ruin two lives —three, if you count mine. And it will achieve nothing.'

'What I have to tell you,' said Henry, 'is that, knowing nothing of the background or the connection with Mrs Barrington, my wife has taken the clipping to London and will undoubtedly have started a newspaper investigation into it. That we can't stop—not now. And if the story becomes public in that way, how can my wife refrain from handing the clipping, or at any rate information about it, to the police?'

Major Sykes stared at him, then put his elbows on to

the edge of the table and silently lowered his face into the palms of his hands. After a moment, Henry rose and left the house, not looking back. What else was there to say, or do?

As he emerged from the lane into the village street, Henry looked carefully both ways; it was a blind corner. He started to crawl out, then thrust on his brake just in time to avoid a car dashing along the street at quite 50, swerving perilously as the driver glanced back to wave cheerfully to him.

'That old man ought to be banned from driving for what remains of his life,' murmured a voice.

Henry, gulping with shock, turned his head and saw Dr Duncan McKay, who had been about to cross the entrance to the lane, standing by his open car window.

'Does Sir Gerald always drive like that?'

'Heaven knows why he hasn't yet hit anything important,' replied the doctor, 'or slain half the village. Everybody's terrified of him once he gets in a car, except Rosa. She often sits beside him, with some splendid hat on top of her head, absolutely unperturbed, no matter what he does, as though she were riding in a carriage and pair.'

'By the way, Doctor, I haven't thanked you properly for the way you looked after my wife, getting her to hospital and all that.'

'Is she all right now?'

'Seems to be. She has gone to London for a conference with her editor.'

'She's a lucky woman, Mr Theobald,' said Dr McKay gravely. 'She moved her head sufficiently for it to be no more than a glancing blow. Had it been direct . . . Well, you saw Sally Clifford's head, the skull actually smashed. The man must be either a maniac or really vicious.'

'It has to be a man?'

'There's little doubt of that. It would take a woman of exceptional strength to strike that sort of blow.'

'Is the husband taking it badly?'

'Very badly indeed. I'm on my way to see him now. Most of the time I'm keeping him under light sedation. Otherwise a breakdown would be inevitable. I'm not sure it isn't anyhow.'

'Seems such a pleasant chap too,' said Henry.

'He is. And he was devoted to Sally.'

'And she to him?' Henry deliberately asked.

The doctor stiffened. 'I suppose they had their difficulties, like most married couples. Well, I must get along. Tell your wife to take things a bit easy for a few days.'

'She won't listen. Thanks once again for taking care of her.'

There seemed to be nobody at home in the Old Rectory, so he decided to go up to his room to jot down everything he could recollect of his talk with Major Sykes. But as he was crossing to the foot of the stairs, he heard Stella's voice through the open door of a small room to one side. 'Was he with you on Monday morning?'

Another woman's voice replied, 'No, why should he be? He has his Victorian Novelists lecture on Monday mornings.'

When she said that, he recognized the voice—Anne Brodie.

'Wait a minute,' she went on. 'I believe he cut that lecture. I don't attend that course—don't agree with Jon on his Victorian views, so I stay away. But somebody told me—Jennifer, I think—that he cancelled the lecture. Said he felt unwell.'

'He was all right by evening. He said nothing to me about being unwell.' There was a long pause. Then Stella's voice came in a low tone. 'Anne, I'm scared.'

'You think . . .?'

'Yes, and so do you.'

Another pause, then the girl's voice: 'It's inconceivable. Not Jon. If it had been only Nick, I'd have been as terrified for him as you are. But Sally Clifford . . . the brutality . . . No, not Jon. It couldn't be.'

Stella, in a voice near to sobs: 'Where was he on Monday morning? I tell you, I'm scared.'

Henry scarcely knew what to do. He shifted cautiously, but a board creaked beneath his foot. He heard a chair move in the room. Scurrying back on tiptoe to the front door, he was just in time to pull it open, as though he had just entered, when Stella came out into the hall.

'Hallo, there,' he said cheerfully.

'Oh, it's you. Have you had lunch?'

'Yes, thanks. Don't bother about me. I've got a brief to study, so I'll slip up to my room.'

'We'll be making a pot of tea in an hour. I'll bring you up a cup.'

'Thanks, that would be kind.'

He went on up. In his room he started to jot down all he could recall of his talk with Major Sykes. But he found it difficult to concentrate. The overheard conversation between the two women, and the strained look on Stella's face down there in the hall, kept intruding into his mind.

After a time he heard his name called. He went to the head of the stairs.

'Henry, it's the phone, for you,' Stella called up. 'It's Mamie Barrington.'

He went down to the phone, intrigued but not unduly surprised.

'This is Mamie Barrington. I've just been talking to Wilfred Sykes. It's important that I see you, Mr Theobald.'

'Of course. When shall I come?'

'Come and have a drink about half past six? Good, I'll expect you.'

Stella told him how to get there. At the far end of the village street turn left, then the second lane on the left.

'Isn't that near Howth Lodge?' he asked.

'Yes, fairly near. Why?'

'Only that I know my way there, so I'll find it all right.'

It was a small modern house, cheaply built, little more than a bungalow with a dormer in the roof. It stood in a small, unkempt garden. The living-room into which she took him was sparsely furnished. All the money, he thought, must go on the bottle; and it looked as though there wasn't much money anyway. Then he remembered there was a boy away at school to be paid for—and a husband in a private hospital. He felt sure it would be a private institution. For all the ravages in her face, she still had a look of pride, of class. He had been an officer, and it was she who would bear the weight of his tragedy, independent of anyone.

Her own gin, half consumed, was already poured. What would he drink? Gin, whisky? He asked if she had a bottle of beer. Yes, there was one somewhere, she replied, finding it in the bottom of a cupboard. Wilfred sometimes drank beer.

They sat opposite each other on hard leather chairs. She began abruptly : 'Wilfred has told me that you know about my husband. Oh, don't waste time on commiseration. I was past that years ago. All that concerns me is Ralph, my son. If he came to know of it, in this sort of way . . . To be brief, he must not. He shall not.'

Her voice was hard and bitter—a woman without any more illusion of happiness, except for her son. She would do anything to protect him. Anything? Henry queried to himself.

'I told Major Sykes,' he said gently, 'that I very much fear your secret is already out of our hands. My wife has started a newspaper enquiry based on the clipping she found in Howth Lodge—not then knowing, of course, that you were in any way involved. Indeed, she still doesn't know. But once you set a newspaper enquiry going, it usually turns up at least a garbled version of the truth. If it does, we are helpless.'

Again she spoke abruptly. 'No newspaper enquiry will find anything to connect me with what happened to my husband. You have stumbled on it by chance. When you mentioned my husband's real name in the bar this morning, you took Wilfred Sykes off his guard. He assumed you had discovered the whole truth, and so revealed it to you.' She gave a short laugh. 'He's been in an agony of repentance ever since. Wilfred is the repentant type. All you have to do is keep quiet, tell nobody, not even your wife. It has nothing to do with anybody except myself.'

She would do anything to protect her son. Had she done that? he wondered. Had there been some moment when Nicholas Bell had threatened to tell her son, and she had picked up the grass shears and struck him? But no, of course that wouldn't do. It was certainly not she who had beaten down Sally Clifford in the cottage on Monday morning. She was nothing like the woman of exceptional strength whom the doctor had stipulated.

'You are asking,' he said, 'for a promise which I have no right to give. It's not a question of telling a newspaper, or my wife. I'm a lawyer, Mrs Barrington. I have even stricter obligations than an ordinary citizen. If I learn anything that may bear upon the commission of a crime, I am bound to inform the police.'

She poured another gulp of gin into her glass. 'I'm a kind of fatalist, Mr Theobald. I believe that there are evil fates that, once set upon a person's life, never loose their hold. Mine began in Malaya. As if that were not enough, they brought me to this village, to the one place in the whole of England where a man lived who knew my secret and was prepared to use it for his own evil amusement.'

'Why did you come here?'

'Because Wilfred already had a house here, and found me this shack which I could afford to buy. And he was the only friend I had.'

'So it was nothing to do with Bell?'

'How could it have been? I knew nothing of him until I lived here. Then one day he asked me to his house and addressed me as Mrs Stallwood.'

'You don't know how he knew?'

'Until Wilfred told me of your talk today, I didn't even know he had the report from the *Straits Times*. How he associated it with me I still don't know.'

'So he wanted money?'

'A little, now and then. What he really wanted was to see me suffer.' She stared at Henry. 'Do you understand what a warped devil Nick Bell was? His pleasure was to inflict pain. Mostly it was his sexual pleasure. No, he wanted nothing of that from me. He wanted only to see a woman suffering for the sake of her son, to twist the screw a little tighter now and then, threaten a little, then relax it, give her hope, before the next tautening. He had a way of laughing . . . . When you and Jonathan Sims came into that room on Friday evening and said he had been killed, a dark cloud rolled off my life.' She was still fixing him with a steady stare. 'Now you propose to roll it over me again, by taking to the police information that has nothing to do with their investigation, nothing to do with anybody except myself, the insane wretch I married, and our son. Does it give you any pleasure to see a woman suffer?'

'That's unfair, Mrs Barrington, and you know it. A man is murdered. He was blackmailing a woman. There's another man in the village who's in love with that woman, and has just discovered what is happening. Could you expect anyone to say there was no possibility that that had anything to do with the killing?'

In a low voice she said, 'Wilfred Sykes did not kill Nick Bell. I am sure of it, and I can prove it.'

'How?'

'I went to the cottage that morning. He had sent for me—one of his usual summonses. When I arrived, he was not in the house. I waited for a while, then wandered into the garden. Then I heard voices from the other side of the wall.'

'From the rose garden beyond, where the greenhouse is?'

'From close to the greenhouse. Two men were quarrelling—or rather, one voice was angry, the other mocking. The angry voice was shouting that he wouldn't get away with it. I didn't hear what it was. The other was mocking him. The mocking voice, of course, was Nick Bell's.'

'And the other?'

'I don't know. I had the impression that I had heard the voice somewhere, but I couldn't place it, perhaps because it was raised in anger. And now, after a lapse of time, I can't even recall it. I should have to hear it again, shouting angrily. And perhaps even then I wouldn't be sure. It was nobody I know well—nobody.'

'What did you do?'

'I walked straight out of the garden and came home. Then, out of relief, Mr Theobald,' she said, smiling wryly, 'I had a drink.'

She got up for another slosh of gin into her glass.

'You have told the police?'

'Of course. I told that fat detective when he interviewed me the same evening. Have another drink?'

'No thanks. I must go. I have to telephone my wife at a fixed time.'

'And your promise?'

'I can't give it,' he told her desperately. 'You know I

can't. I'll do all I can to keep your secret, but I can't promise. I'll have to see what happens before I decide.'

On the way back to the Old Rectory he felt reasonably sure he knew what had happened. But he would wait to talk to Kate before he did anything.

He was sleeping soundly when the noise started.

Kate had not telephoned him, so earlier in the evening he had tried to reach her, but the office said she had gone out to dinner with some of the lads. He had wandered along to the Nag's Head for a few beers, a sandwich, a few more beers. So he was sleeping soundly when the noise at last roused him—knocking on his door, and Jonathan's voice : 'Henry, you're wanted on the phone.'

'At this hour,' he muttered, switching on the light, groping for his dressing-gown, glancing at his watch. It was 1.35 in the morning. 'My dear fellow,' he apologized to Jonathan, opening the door, 'I'm terribly sorry you've been woken like this. Who is it?'

'Kate's newspaper.'

'Oh, the hell with them,' he grumbled, going downstairs. 'Why can't they keep reasonable hours like anybody else? Hallo, yes. Theobald here. What is it?'

Butch's voice : 'Henry, it's all right. Don't be alarmed. Kate is all right now. But there has been an accident.'

'Tell me quickly.'

'We all went out on a celebration dinner and got a bit plastered. We saw her home to your flat, safe and sound. She must have decided to boil herself some milk, and then gone to bed and forgotten about it. The milk boiled over and put out the gas burner on the cooker. No, I tell you, she's all right. The flat filled with gas, but she woke because it choked her, just in time to get to the window and open it. She tried to shout. Luckily a policeman happened to be on patrol in the street below. He broke open the flat door and got her out of it. She's all right. But I blame myself, old man. I blame myself like hell. It was my fault, getting us all drunk . . .'

'Where is she?'

'Back in the flat, in bed, with a girl from the office looking after her. She's okay now.'

'Tell her I'm starting right away. It'll take me about a couple of hours to drive there.'

'I'll be waiting at the flat,' promised Butch. 'But don't worry. She's all right now.'

CHAPTER XII

KATE WAS STILL in bed. Henry was in the kitchen, chivvying buttered eggs round the pan for her and watching the coffee percolate. She still felt sick and could eat little, although their doctor had pronounced her unharmed except for a sore throat; so the girl from the office had been sent home with expressions of warm gratitude.

'Seems to be some point in having a husband after all,' murmured Kate as he came in with the tray. 'Darling, do you think I can really eat this?'

'Do you good, the doc says.'

She ate a little, then gestured to him to take away the tray. All she could take was a few sips of coffee.

'What bothers me,' she told him, her voice still rasping, 'is that I can't remember putting on milk to boil. I don't think I did. I know I was fairly well lit, but why should I boil milk? I loathe boiled milk. In fact, as you know, I loathe boiled anything.'

'You must have done. What other explanation could there be?'

'And why was the bedroom window shut,' she mused. 'I'm pretty damn sure I opened it. I always open the bedroom window before I get into bed—or tell you to. When one's in alcohol, one doesn't forget ingrained habits. Correct?'

Henry shrugged. 'One is, I think, unpredictable, wouldn't one say?'

'I'm damn sure I wouldn't have put any milk on to boil,' she suddenly asserted decisively, 'and I'm certain I opened the bedroom window.'

Henry looked at her over his coffee cup. 'Do you mean that somebody else did? Was anybody else with you? Should I be working up into a dudgeon?'

'I brought some of the biggest drunks in Fleet Street home with me, but they all dispersed. There was no attempt, to the best of my recollection, on our marriage bed. All the same, I didn't either boil milk or forget to open the window.'

'Then who?'

'Somebody who thought I was finding out too much?'

'Oh, but that's ridiculous.'

'Is it? I've been breaking a lot in the *Post*. Suppose I'd stumbled on something, perhaps even without realizing its importance. Anybody who knew I was coming to London alone could easily have found our address in the phone book. So they watch. So I come home, very merry, and a cinch to drop into a stupor directly I get into bed. So they wait a bit, then break in—anybody could force that night latch . . .'

'Didn't you put the safety chain on?'

'I couldn't have done, or the policeman who heard me shout couldn't have broken in later. And he found the front door of the whole building open.'

'Butch could have left it open after he delivered you home.'

'Sure. But it makes it easier for my night visitor to break in. He looks into the bedroom. Madam is snoring. He closes the window, leaves the bedroom door ajar, boils a saucepan of milk on the gas cooker in the kitchen, lets it boil over, leaves the gas turned on and quietly lets himself out. What could be safer? Everybody knows I came in as tight as a tick. I was even past finding a night-dress to put on—lying there naked. So I was careless. So I was dead.'

Henry leaned over to hold her hand. 'So you're alive and well. But we can check it, you know. If anybody broke in, there'll be marks on the door.'

'No go, darling. A policeman broke in later—and certainly didn't pause to see if there were any marks on the door before he made a few of his own.'

For a couple of minutes they both sat in silence, thinking it over. At last Henry put the obvious questions: 'Who, then?'

'Dr Wisbech was on the London train with me yesterday. Could have been just coincidence, of course. He said he was going to the Rose Show, and in fact did—one of our lads tried to interview him there. But we had an interesting little chat on the train, and he let one thing slip. He knew the blue rose plants had been shifted, although he pretended not to know what had happened to them.'

The phone rang. It was one of the early-shift men on the news desk. Yes, Kate assured him, she was all right. No, she had not yet seen this morning's paper, because they'd cancelled the regular order when they went off to Ashworth. She'd send Henry out directly to buy one from round the corner.

The news desk assured her it was a glowing front page. 'And, Kate, there's been a very angry Detective-Inspector Kippis on the blower. He's furious that you broke Bell's real identity in the *Post* this morning.'

Kate crowed with pleasure. 'The Tom Stevens who did 2 years for robbery with violence? So our guess was right? Good on us! Then we must also be right about

Tom Stevens, the con man in Malay. That's what led to Tom Stevens, the robber.'

The lawyer, he told her, had got cold feet at the last minute, and had insisted on holding over that part of her story until he got confirmation from the stringer in Kuala Lumpur that there wasn't still a well-known Malayan resident named Tom Stevens, now a flourishing and highly respected merchant banker or some damn thing. The foreign editor had put the Singapore stringer on to it too. Nothing had yet come from either. The poor devils, as the foreign editor had pointed out, had been roused from their sleep, or whatever else they were doing in bed, in their own small hours, and had no doubt been scurrying about ever since.

'We ought to get something from both of them by early afternoon,' the news desk went on. 'Unless they produce a current Tom Stevens in Malay, the lawyer's willing to let your piece through for tomorrow, and chance it. So we shan't have to bother you for anything today.'

'And if there is a current Tom Stevens?'

'Don't worry. We've sent young Bob Ritchie to Linchester to cover for you until you get back. So take it easy. He can stay on and do the legwork if you like.'

Kate grunted approval. She had worked with Bob when she had been on a story in Scotland, before they brought him from the Glasgow office to London. Very reliable and a strong support he had proved. And a very handsome young man, Bob Ritchie.

'By the way,' said the news desk, 'reverting to Detective-Inspector Kippis. He demanded to know where you got the information about Tom Stevens, and Roger Wake wants to see you urgently.'

'What did you tell 'em?'

'I said a newspaper never reveals its sources—to which the Detective-Inspector replied balls—and that you were in a delicate state of health.'

'Quite right,' said Kate, 'although I could have wished you had phrased it differently.'

She was up and dressed for lunch, in spite of Henry's pleading. She had insisted that she was quite recovered. Very well then, he would take her out to lunch—somewhere quiet, but rather smart. At that she had paled. All she really fancied was another helping of those delicious buttered eggs, two thin slices of wholemeal toast and perhaps a tiny little brandy and soda as a restorative—just a small double.

Afterwards, as they settled into their armchairs with cups of coffee, she said, 'Let's swap news.'

She told him of her day of discoveries at the office, and he told her of his enquiries at Ashworth while she had been away.

Kate pondered. 'I take it we can rule out Billy Tooth, the retired comic.'

'If there was any money lying about, I think he might have whipped it. I'm sure he was telling me the truth about the post-dated cheques, and he didn't find them. I don't think he has the guts to have murdered Bell for them—although there's always the possibility, with Tooth or anyone else, of the hasty blow struck in a sudden burst of rage. But I agree—rule him out.'

'So next we have Jonathan Sims again.'

'I doubt it,' replied Henry. 'After all, what additional information have we? By an overheard conversation, we know that Jonathan cut a lecture he was supposed to give on Monday morning, so presumably might have been at Howth Lodge at the time Sally Clifford was killed and you were knocked out. We also know that his wife and his girl friend are scared for him. But what does that prove? Nothing, except that they are apprehensive. This girl Anne Brodie was deeply involved with Bell, and automatically feels guilty. Stella knows that he's a moody, difficult man who might be capable, in a rage, of killing. But why on earth should he then have killed Sally Clifford? Because she interrupted his search of the cottage? I don't believe that, even if she had, he would have smashed her skull in. And, anyway, what would he have been searching for? It doesn't make sense.'

'Then what does?'

'Mamie Barrington, I'm afraid,' he answered sadly.

'Oh come,' protested Kate, 'it was no female alcoholic who knocked me out in Bell's bedroom.'

'Mamie Barrington and Wilfred Sykes, who's in love with her. Can't you see how the whole thing pathetically fits? Bell tells Mamie to come to his house that morning. The blackmail will go on. He isn't in the house. She finds him in his greenhouse. He makes some mocking threat which she can no longer tolerate—perhaps says that the time has come to tell her son about his father, directly he returns for the school holidays. She pleads. He jeers and turns away to get on with the rose he is pollinating. She snatches up the grass shears lying on the bench, thrusts into his throat.'

'Why did she then substitute the knife in the wound, if the grass shears were his? And they must have been his. She wouldn't have gone to that sort of meeting in her gardening jacket. Anyway, you say she doesn't seem to do any gardening.'

'She realized that her fingerprints would be on the shears. So she picked up a knife, using a piece of rag or something, to substitute; then took the shears away to lose.'

'Sounds too cold-blooded for a woman,' hazarded Kate.

'You haven't had a close look at Mamie. Like a tiger with her cub. And she's highly intelligent—quick-brained enough, in spite of the alcohol, to work out coolly about the fingerprints after she had struck the blow, with the man sagging across the greenhouse bench in front of her.'

'Lummee!' said Kate, impressed.

'When I met her yesterday, it became clear towards the end of our talk that she wasn't really trying to head us off from the Malayan story for publicity reasons, or even for the sake of her son. She wants to, of course. But her main object, which she approached cunningly, was to tell me that she had overheard Bell and another man, whose voice she did not recognize, quarrelling loudly in the greenhouse. I don't believe it. If I had her in the witness box, I'd shake her out of that tale inside 10 minutes. At the very least, she'd have peeped through that door in the garden wall, to see who was quarrelling with the man she hated.'

'She said she told the police about it the same day.'

'And I bet Roger Wake doesn't believe it either.'

'But he told me there'd been somebody at Howth Lodge that morning who hadn't come forward.'

'He certainly didn't mean Mamie Barrington's phantom quarreller. He warned you of the danger of discovering who the person was. Not a phantom, darling. He meant somebody else.'

Kate pondered, then had to agree that it fitted. And then, she supposed, Mamie had told Wilfred Sykes. So it was he who had been searching the cottage on Monday morning. What for?

'For whatever evidence Bell might have had,' suggested Henry, 'on which he was blackmailing her. I doubt if they even knew what they were looking for. But they had to find it, in case the police should, and it would incriminate Mamie. They! I've just realized. When I thought I heard somebody in the garden, there was somebody there. Mamie. It was she who got away over the wall. Sykes was still in the cottage. He had struck down Sally Clifford in a panic, probably not meaning to kill her, just stun her, with whatever he happened to be holding—a poker, maybe, or some wrench with which he had been tearing at the walls. And then he saw she was dead. And we came in. He's a cool chap, a soldier, trained for emergencies. If he panicked over Sally Clifford, maybe it was because she had seen Mamie and cried out. But he quickly recovered his nerve. He hid in the bedroom, waiting for us to rush from the house to fetch help for Sally Clifford. Unexpectedly, you went upstairs. So he struck you down—not savagely or wildly, not meaning to kill you, only to knock you out for long enough to get away. It fits. Poor devils! She had reason to speak of being dogged by an evil fate.'

CHAPTER XIII

As THEY CAME on to the crest of the hill at the end of Linchester High Street, when Henry drove her down there next morning, Kate gazed across the valley at the university buildings and the straggling village beyond. 'Looks dreamy enough.'

From this distance the village was largely clothed in the lushness of oaks, elms and ash trees, with dull red chimneys or thatched roofs emerging here and there. It seemed grotesquely incongruous that in such a sleepy valley had lived a man whose pleasure lay in tormenting women and who had paid for it with a blade thrust into his throat, and another who had crushed a woman's skull with a blow struck as though by a maniac. 'We must get on with it as fast as we can,' she murmured almost to herself.

'Take it easy for another 24 hours,' urged Henry.

'No, I'm all right.' The day's rest in their little flat in Chelsea, and one good night's sleep with Henry snoring contentedly beside her, had restored her. The cure was complete when she picked up the *Post* in the morning. Her story of Tom Stevens, the con man in Malaya, occupied most of page one. The two stringers had come through in time, with enough to reassure the lawyer. Not only was there no current and respectable Tom Stevens in Malaysia, but 15 years ago Tom Stevens had been arrested on a charge of conspiracy to defraud. He had skipped his bail and never since been found. Always it had been assumed that he had got out of the country, but Interpol had never succeeded in picking him up. There could be little doubt now of the chain—Tom Stevens, having served his sentence in England for robbery with violence, quietly gets away to the Far East. Next he turns up in Malaya and is caught for some sort of property fraud. He jumps his bail, skips out of the country and vanishes. So far, Kate pondered, nobody knew where he had been for the next 7 years. But then he turns up in Ashworth under the name of Nicholas Bell and settles at Howth Lodge in apparent affluence. Where had the money come from? Presumably from the Malayan fraud. She must get the stringers working harder on that. She needed to know if the fraud had been completed, and whether Tom Stevens was thought to have got away with the proceeds—and how much was involved.

As they passed the university, Henry broke in on her. 'We ought to take that newspaper clipping to Wake right away.'

'It's not an interview I'm looking forward to keenly.'

'I'll take it to him if you like.'

'No, I'll give it to him when he summonses me to grill me about our Tom Stevens stories. Maybe it'll mollify him a bit.'

'Shall I drive you back to Linchester, then, when we've dropped our bags at the Old Rectory?'

Kate shook her head. 'Let's wait until Wake sends for me, darling. And Henry, meanwhile there is something. I keep on remembering what Wake said, when I met him at the flower show, about somebody else being at Howth Lodge that morning who hadn't come forward. Let's have another go at that.'

'How?'

'Just the way we started—going to see the people we know were there, and must have told the police they were.'

'Well, I started that with Mamie Barrington, and all I got out of her was an obvious fabrication.'

'I'm not so sure,' mused Kate. 'It's only a fabrication on the assumption that Mamie killed Bell, and Sykes killed Sally Clifford. But suppose we're wrong about that. Then she would have no reason to try to fob you off—and the police too—with an imaginary overheard quarrel. If she's telling the truth, then the phantom quarreller may be the man Wake was talking about. But it's no use going back to her. She won't say any more.'

'Then who?'

'Let's start again where we started originally. Sir Gerald Hawkes was there. You go to see him—you can find some excuse about roses or something. Nellie Cordoni was watching, even if she wasn't actually there. I'll go to see her. Maybe, now that we know exactly what we're trying to find out, we can pick up a lead from one or the other.'

'How about Billy Tooth? He was there too.'

'Later, perhaps. I don't have a hunch about Billy Tooth.'

'You're the boss,' he said resignedly.

Nellie Cordoni was in. Kate caught a glimpse of her behind the windowsill geraniums as Henry stopped the car outside her cottage. 'I'll leave you the car,' he said, 'and walk round to Sir Gerald's. I'd like a stretch. See you at the Old Rectory in about an hour.'

As Kate approached the cottage door, Nellie Cordoni emerged, scarf round head, shopping basket over arm. She wore them, thought Kate, like a gossip's uniform.

'Mrs Theobald, how nice to see you. I was just off to do a little shopping. But never mind. Do come in.'

Kate took the proffered chair by the french window to the rear garden. The large grey cat was again sleeping in the sun on the stone path outside, as though it never did anything else.

'I've been reading your wonderful write-ups in the newspaper,' began Nellie. 'How clever you are, finding out all that. Just to think, Nick Bell living among us all those years, friendly with us all, and nobody suspecting for a moment that he was a criminal. And then you find it out in a few days! But it's awful, isn't it my dear, to think how little one knows about one's closest neighbours.'

Kate laughed pleasantly. 'It must have been a great surprise to you, Mrs Cordoni.'

'It was, my dear, I assure you. And the same about poor Sally Clifford. Nobody dreamed that she was, how shall I say, involved with that dreadful man.'

'You think she was, then?'

'No doubt of it, surely. I mean, why go back into that cottage at all, unless she had good reason.'

'She was supposed to have gone to look for an earring she thought she had dropped on Friday evening, when we were all there.'

Mrs Cordoni raised her eyebrows, sufficient comment. 'All that sham about horse-riding.'

'Sham?'

'Every day, when she was supposed to be out horse-riding . . . It's clear now where she rode her horse to. Sneaking into Bell's garden by the back way . . .'

'You mean, if she had gone in the front, you'd have seen her?'

'Well, I'd have been bound to, my dear, wouldn't I?'

'Geraniums need so much attention,' murmured Kate.

'It's poor Jack I'm sorry for,' the gossip went on. 'Quite broken up by it all. Stuck away in that house of his, with nobody to look after him, except when Dr McKay goes in once a day. Why doesn't that daughter of his come home to care for him? That's what I'd like to know. Selfish little hussy! But then, all the young seem to be like that these days, nothing but self, and going about half naked, and no morals at all to speak of. I mean, what are we all coming to?'

At least, thought Kate, Nellie Cordoni had not yet picked up that piece of gossip, and Kate was certainly not going to hand it to her.

'I met Dr Wisbech on the train to London,' she threw in as a diversion. 'He was going to the Rose Show.'

'And there's another one,' said Nellie darkly, 'suffering from another person's selfishness—and, come to that, morals, to be frank.'

'His wife?'

'Gone to a sanatorium in Switzerland.'

'Dr Wisbech told me she has a rather serious form of anaemia.'

'Anaemia! I've heard of folk going to a sanatorium in Switzerland for lung troubles. Have you ever heard of anyone going there for anaemia? Rubbish. What he's trying to get her cured of has nothing to do with her blood.'

'You mean, she's gone to a drug clinic?'

'Never mind what I mean, my dear. I know when to keep my thoughts to myself. There's some that think Dr Wisbech wouldn't very much care if she never came back from the sanatorium.'

'He has other interests?'

'That's not for me to say. You should ask Mr Sims's girl friend, if you want that kind of information.'

'Anne Brodie?'

'Mind you, it's not I who say so. But one hears things now and then.'

It didn't make sense, thought Kate. Nellie had already slipped her one nonsense about Anne being Jonathan's mistress. Now she was bedding her down with Wisbech. Yet the truth, all the time, was that she was enmeshed with Nick Bell; the one thing Nellie did not know about. Kate had no reservations about that. It came from Jonathan himself. He would not have invented so painful a lie.

'Another interesting thing I heard about Dr Wisbech too,' Nellie Cordoni went brightly on. 'You discovered that Nick Bell was a criminal. Dr Wisbech, it seems, was not all that he should have been either.'

'What do you mean?'

'He was mixed up in a scandal over a property deal. It was in one of the South American countries—something to do with buying up cattle ranches and developing them. Sir Gerald knows all about it. I happened to meet him out shopping earlier this morning. He said it was your write-up in the paper about a property scandal in Malaya that recalled it to his memory. He was in the consular service in South America at the time. Dr Wisbech was supposed to be there for a scientific expedition. But, according to Sir Gerald, that wasn't his main idea at all. Mind you, no charge was ever brought against him, Sir Gerald says. Apparently there was some covering-up in official circles, because he was a well-known British scientist. But it was generally talked about, and Dr Wisbech had to leave the country hurriedly.'

'Did Sir Gerald say when all this was?'

'Oh, about 10 or 11 years ago, I think he said.'

Kate was calculating hurriedly. That put it right in

the middle of the 7 years during which they knew nothing of what had happened to Tom Stevens, after he had slipped his bail, on a charge of fraudulent property deals in Malaya, and before he turned up in Ashworth as Nicholas Bell.

It seemed to Henry, as he walked round to Sir Gerald's farmhouse in Pinchback lane, that he was unlikely to get anything out of the old man unless he took him by surprise, and bluffed. So he avoided the front of the house and made his way round to the garden. On such a fine day there was a good chance that Sir Gerald would be among his roses.

As he was. In a pair of canvas slacks, a pale pink shirt open at the neck, an old straw hat and sandals, he was pottering about, as Henry was sure he would put it, in the greenish light of his shaded greenhouse. He had evidently just pollinated the rose on the bench before him, and was carefully writing the necessary records in a large, leather-bound manuscript book.

When Henry coughed, he swung round with a little cry. 'Dear me, Mr Theobald, how you startled me!'

'So sorry.'

'I was absorbed in my rose nonsense.' He emitted his habitual high-pitched chuckle. Already he was recovering equanimity. The professionally charming smile was already returning to his long, thin, distinguished-looking face. 'Everybody is so bored with me about it, that I don't expect to find somebody coming into the garden.'

'I should apologize,' said Henry deferentially, 'but it was deliberate, sir.'

'Deliberate?'

'I didn't want to worry Lady Hawkes with my visit.'

'Worry?'

Henry leaned slowly against the jamb of the greenhouse door. He was imagining the old man in the witness box, and he himself, in wig and gown, rising slowly to begin his cross-examination. 'There's probably nothing in it after all. But I felt I ought to put it to you privately.'

'What is this all about?' asked Sir Gerald.

Henry wished he could think that the perspiration on the old man's face and in the hollow of his thin neck was caused by anxiety, rather than the heat and humidity inside the greenhouse.

'At about 1 o'clock on the day that Nicholas Bell was killed, Sir Gerald, you drove up to his cottage and stopped so abruptly that the squeal of your brakes attracted attention. Do you always drive like that, by the way? You nearly got me in the village street a couple of days ago.'

The old man tittered. And that, Henry noted with satisfaction, was a nervous reaction. 'The people in the village are always pulling my leg about my driving. But they mistake for rashness what is really consummate skill. My licence, like my conscience, is clean.'

'I diverged,' said Henry. 'Mrs Cordoni, attracted to her window by the squeal of your brakes, saw you nip into the gate of Howth Lodge and come out again after only a few minutes to drive off at the same consummately skilful speed. She thought you were just leaving a note to say you and Lady Hawkes would come to drinks that evening. But my wife, who has been making enquiries for her newspaper, has been told that there was a different reason for the briefness of your visit.'

'Told by whom?' There was a sharpness now in his voice. For a moment the smile was no longer there.

'She wouldn't disclose that, even to me. It's a point of honour with newspaper people. What she was told was that either you saw something you wish you had not seen, or somebody you did not wish to be seen by.'

There was a long silence. The old man began to fiddle nervously with the pen he still held in his hand; then, realizing he was doing so, put it down on the book.

'Which was it, Sir Gerald?' asked Henry softly.

He was jubilant inside himself. The long shot had hit the target. And it was a reasonable guess what that target was. He paused for a few moments, then, as the other said nothing, continued, 'The police know that there was a visitor to Howth Lodge that day who has not come forward. They dearly want to discover who it was. You know, don't you, Sir Gerald? You saw him, and quickly left the place before he saw you. Why haven't you told the police about it?'

'Out of pity for him. It had nothing to do with Bell's murder.' He sighed. 'But if somebody now knows that I saw him, I suppose I must go to the police and own up.'

'How can you possibly know it was nothing to do with Bell's murder?'

'When you enter the front gate of Howth Lodge, you look straight across the garden to the door in the far wall. If that is open, you can see into the paddock beyond, where Nicky Bell planted out most of his roses, and where his greenhouse is—though, of course, you can't see that, for it's built against the other side of the wall.'

'And the door was open? So you could see into the paddock? What was it you saw?'

'He was digging up rose plants from a row near the middle.'

Henry gazed hard at him and asked with deliberation, 'Do you know, Sir Gerald, that Bell's blue roses have been removed from where he planted them?'

'I guessed as much. If anybody was going to steal rose plants from Nick Bell's garden, those would be the ones he'd want.'

Henry was trying to clarify his thoughts without seeming to. It had to be somebody who knew which rose plants to take. In effect, it had to be Wisbech. Hadn't Sir Gerald said, the first time Henry interviewed him, that Bell had allowed nobody to see his blue rose? But that, of course, would not apply to his partner in the hybridization. Wisbech would know where the plants were.

'Why,' he asked slowly, 'do you say with such assurance that it had nothing to do with Bell's murder?'

The old man tittered again. 'My dear Mr Theobald, can you imagine anybody calmly digging up roses if a man's corpse were lying covered in blood in the garden?'

'Suppose the man digging up the roses had just killed Bell.'

'Really, let's be sensible. Would anybody who had just killed a friend in a violent quarrel think of anything except getting away? He certainly would not pause to dig up roses, you can be sure of that.'

'Then where was Bell at the time?'

'I have no idea. Perhaps he was out on some errand and the thief knew of it and took his chance to get the roses. Perhaps he was in the cottage having his lunch. I didn't go in. The thing was nothing to do with me. I wanted to know nothing about it—nothing at all.'

It was still not fitting. There was still something wrong, but Henry could not for the moment identify it.

'If it had nothing to do with the murder, why hasn't he come forward to the police?'

'For that very reason, I should say, Mr Theobald. He could not assist the police in any consequential way in their enquiries, so why should he admit to a theft—and lose the possibility of a fortune?'

The flaw, Henry suddenly saw, was that it was too risky for anybody to venture into the paddock to dig up the roses, without even shutting the door in the garden wall, if Bell was in the cottage having his lunch. He might have stepped out into the garden at any time.

Even if Wisbech knew he was out, he might have returned unexpectedly. So was Sir Gerald lying?

'Perhaps,' said Henry, 'he was entitled to dig up the plants. Perhaps Bell had arranged for him to do so. After all, they were in some sort of partnership.'

'Were they?' asked Sir Gerald, surprised.

'It was you yourself who told me that Bell and Dr Wisbech worked together to produce the blue rose.'

'Dr Wisbech? I am not speaking of Dr Wisbech.'

'Then who?'

'The man I saw in Bell's paddock was Jack Clifford.'

Kate was already at the Old Rectory by the time he got there. 'Listen, darling, I got something rather odd from Nellie.'

'So did I from old Hawkes. Tell me yours first.'

She told him what Nellie Cordoni had said of Wisbech being involved in a property fraud in South America. If they had guessed right about Tom Stevens, the con man in Malaya, it seemed a very odd coincidence. Didn't it look rather as though Stevens, as Bell was then named, had skipped from Malaya to South America, started the same sort of game there, and Wisbech had been mixed up in it? So didn't it look as though there had been a paying-off of old scores? 'I always thought Dr Wisbech was out of focus, if you see what I mean.'

'Not convinced,' Henry disagreed. 'It's very curious the way Wisbech keeps on cropping up, and then it turns out to be wrong after all. First there was the suggestion that his wife's on drugs, and Bell was the supplier. I'm sure that was nonsense. Then there was your idea that he was the man who broke into your flat and tried to gas you in your sleep. And, frankly, I think that's nonsense too. Why should he want to? And if, for some reason we can't get at, he did want to get rid of you, it's so unlikely he'd pick on that method.'

'He was the only one of them in London.'

'So far as we know. And it means nothing at all.'

'You think I really did put milk on to boil, and the whole thing was just my damn stupidity.'

'To put it no higher, it's a possibility, isn't it darling? And even if there was an attempt,' he hurried on, ducking the argument in her look, 'there's absolutely nothing to link it with Wisbech. And then there was your suspicion, from your talk with him on the train, that he was the chap who'd taken the blue roses. And that's wrong too.' He told her of his questioning of Sir Gerald. 'So that turns out not to be Wisbech either, but Jack Clifford.'

'Jack Clifford,' she murmured, pondering.

'What puzzles me,' he added, 'is how Clifford could have known which were the blue rose plants.'

Kate got up abruptly. 'Let's go and ask him. Let's go now.'

'In spite of Wake's warning?'

'Oh, don't be silly, sweetheart. What danger could there possibly be from poor old Jack Clifford, who's had his life torn to bits and is drinking himself into oblivion?'

Clifford's Rose Nurseries lay about a mile beyond the village. At the entrance gate stood a small wooden office backing on to banks of greenhouses whitewashed over as protection from the sun. Flanking the road behind a wire fence, and stretching far beyond the greenhouses, were the roses planted out to grow on for sale—several acres of them, blooming sumptuously, row crowded upon magnificent row of scarlet, yellow, deep pink, white, crimson, splashed on the scene like paint scraped thickly on to the canvas with a palette knife. And in the still air the delicate, unobtrusive, inescapable fragrance.

There was nobody in the office. Three gardeners were working at widely separated points among the roses.

Otherwise the place was unpeopled. Kate drove up the central roadway of the nursery, reckoning the house must be somewhere at the rear.

One of the gardeners stepped into the roadway. Kate stopped. 'We've come to see Mr Clifford. Is he at the house?'

The man nodded and gestured his thumb away to the left.

'Dr McKay told me he had him under sedation a couple of days ago,' said Henry. 'Is he all right to be visited now?'

'Reckon so. Doctor took him off the drugs yesterday. Inquest was yesterday.'

Kate asked, 'How has Mr Clifford taken it?'

The gardener shrugged. 'Same as before, only worse.'

'Ah well, poor chap,' said Kate, rolling the car forward again.

After a pause, Henry asked if she thought it worth going on. Why not? she argued. If Clifford were insensibly drunk, they'd have lost nothing. On the other hand, he might just be at the talkative stage.

'Intrusion on privacy,' he murmured. 'Kate, I don't like it. If he's at all reluctant, we just make polite excuses and leave.'

'Sure. I've no desire to be up before the Press Council.'

'Nor I before the Bar Council.'

The house lay behind a tall bank of shrubs and trees. It was a pleasant brick house with white clapboarding on the upper parts and a white porch overgrown with purple clematis. Henry rang the bell and waited; rang it again and waited. Silence. He returned to the car. 'It's no good, darling. We'd better leave it.'

But her expression changed and she nodded her head over his shoulder. He turned to see the door open and Jack Clifford, unshaven, in pyjamas and an old silk dressing-gown, standing in the porch.

Kate was out of the car and over to him. 'Theobalds, Mr Clifford. The people stayed with Jonathan and Stella Sims. I meant to come before to express our sympathy on your loss, but I myself was attacked, as you know, and then I've had to be in London.'

At first Henry thought the man would turn her off. But suddenly he began to babble. She had been loved by everyone—by everyone. Tears were appearing on his cheeks. Kate had been right—the talkative stage.

Suddenly he snapped into a different mood. 'You were the two who found her, eh? Tell me. I want to know. Tell me.'

'She couldn't have suffered, Mr Clifford,' said Kate evenly. 'She was struck one terrible blow. She must have died instantly. She couldn't have suffered.'

He reached forward and took her hand. 'Come in, come in.' He was weeping now. 'Come in. Come in and tell me.'

He took them to the wide, stone-flagged kitchen where he had been sitting in an old rocking-chair with a blanket thrown across it; and on the table beside him a glass and a half-empty bottle of gin. 'Have a drink.'

Kate saw an electric percolator on the work surface. 'I'd love some coffee. Let me make you some too. And get you something to eat.'

He nodded sympathetically, trusting her. She found a tin of coffee on the shelf above, and in the fridge were 12 pints of milk (he hadn't bothered to cancel the daily order) and some eggs. Kate whipped four eggs into a bowl to scramble, started the percolater, thrust slices of bread under the cooker grill to toast.

While she was at it, Clifford sat down opposite Henry at the kitchen table and went on babbling about his wife, sentimental, almost maudlin. Then he suddenly snapped again. 'Betty isn't here,' he said in a loud voice. 'Her mother dead, and Betty isn't here.'

Henry murmured sympathetically: 'She's in hospital in London, I understand.'

Clifford gave him a contemptuous look. 'Why don't you say what you mean? Newspaper folk, eh? If you say that, you know she's in an abortion clinic. Fifteen years of age, still at school . . .'

He made a grab for the gin bottle. But Kate took it deftly from his hand and put the coffee and the eggs-on-toast before him. He looked up tremulously at her. Then, after a hesitant start, ate greedily. How long, she wondered, since he had last eaten?

After a few minutes he seemed to have sobered considerably, so she ventured: 'Mr Clifford, what I'm trying to do is to help, so far as a newspaper organization can, to find out who committed these awful murders—first Nick Bell, then your wife. That's my aim.'

He nodded again. He seemed to have taken to her as a distressed child might in its misery.

'One line we've been following,' she went on, 'is the story that Nick Bell had bred a blue rose.'

'So he did. I saw it. He showed me the plants a couple of weeks before he was killed. One had a single bloom on it, the others only buds, rather small. The bloom was a wonderful blue. Nick cut it off and put it in his pocket. Now that I'd seen it, he said, he wasn't taking any chances.'

Now Henry ventured: 'Mr Clifford, the blue rose plants have been dug from Bell's paddock and removed. Did you know that?'

'Of course I did. I dug 'em. It's what we arranged a couple of weeks before. That's why he showed me the one in bloom. He wanted them budded on to as much stock as possible, and he was scared to do the job himself. He reckoned it ought to be done by a professional, because the rose was too valuable to take risks with. And he was right. There's a fortune in that rose. So on Friday—early in the afternoon of the day he got killed —I went round, as arranged, to pick out the roses and bring them back here. I've got them planted here now.'

'Where was Bell while you were in the garden?'

'How should I know. In his cottage, probably. It was lunch time.'

'Didn't it occur to you,' asked Henry slowly, 'that, after Bell had been murdered, you ought to have gone to the police with all that information?'

Clifford grunted. 'Of course it occurred to me. But then something else occurred to me. Nobody knew I had the roses. They'd nothing to do with Nick's death. All I had to do was bud them privately, keep them a few years, then produce a few for trials. I'd be rich for life. So why should I go to the police? That's what occurred to me, Mr Theobald.'

'They might suspect you of killing Bell in order to steal his rose.'

A look of shrewdness came into his eyes, bleary though they were with alcohol. 'They'd not be likely to do that unless they knew about the rose, eh? And how would they know about it, unless I told 'em. Gossip? What does that amount to? When all the roses in Nick's garden bloomed, and none of 'em was blue, who'd believe the gossip—so long as I didn't tell the police.'

'Then why,' asked Henry bluntly, 'are you telling us?'

Clifford stared at him, then got up from his chair, steadied himself against the table and made for the back door. 'Come on. I'll show you why I'm telling you. Come on.'

The door led into a small walled garden, the private garden of the house. It was badly cared for. Professionals don't garden for fun.

At the far end a small area had been fenced off with

wattle. Behind it, 6 rose plants had been sunk in their pots into the soil. Two carried blooms. The opening buds were deep purple, fading to pale lavender on the blooms that were fully out.

'That's why I'm telling you now,' said Clifford. 'There's no longer any point in it.'

'These were the plants you took from Bell's garden? So they didn't come true? The blue rose he showed you was just a freak and the bushes have reverted to lavender?'

Clifford shook his head. 'No, Mr Theobald. Roses don't behave like that—they're not rhododendrons or lupins. Nick had 6 plants of genuine blue roses all right. But these aren't the same plants.'

'You mean you dug up from the wrong position?'

He shook his head again. 'I took 'em from the right place. But between the time Nick showed me the blue bloom, and the day I dug up the plants, they'd been switched—other plants substituted.' He bent over and held the stem of one in his hand. 'It's a clever switch. Look at those leaves—practically identical. There's Baby Faurax in those plants, or something similar. They were like enough to fool me, even when I got the plants back here—until they bloomed. Then it was obvious. They'd been switched.'

'Switched by Bell himself, do you think?' asked Henry, puzzled.

'There'd be no point in that,' broke in Kate.

Clifford turned his faithful-dog gaze on her and agreed. 'You're right. All he had to do was tell me he'd changed his mind.'

'Then who?' asked Henry.

Clifford shrugged. 'But we'll know soon enough. The moment someone comes up with a genuine pale blue rose, that's him.'

Henry stared, cursing himself silently. For, of course,

he knew already; should have known long before. Two blue roses produced simultaneously in the same village was a coincidence so wild as to be virtually impossible. And he'd been too stupid to see it.

CHAPTER XIV

KATE DROPPED HENRY at the corner of Pinchback lane. He wanted to go back to see old Hawkes. He would not say why—just that there was something he had forgotten to ask him. Then she drove on to the Old Rectory.

A police car was standing outside. A sergeant got out as soon as she drew up. 'Chief Superintendent's compliments, and he'd like to see you as soon as convenient.'

'Meaning now?'

'Meaning now. If you like to go in your own car, we'll follow. He's at the police station in Linchester.'

Roger Wake was seated at a littered desk in a small office at the rear. When she sat opposite him, he picked out from his in-tray clippings of her *Post* stories that morning and the previous day. 'Sources please, Mrs Theobald.'

'You know how pig-headed newspapers are about revealing sources, Mr Wake.'

'This is a matter of the utmost seriousness. I need to know who told you Bell's real name, and who put you on to his activities in Malaya. I'm not going to bring up the possibility of the Director of Public Prosecutions. I'm simply going to remind you that this is a murder investigation, and give you my word that there is grave risk of further attempts on life, including your own. Who told you?'

'Now you'll think I'm giving you the information because you've scared me—and you'll be right!' She laughed. 'Honestly, Mr Wake, I was going to tell you anyway, first chance I got, which is now. Nobody told me.' She fidgeted in her handbag for the clipping from the *Straits Times*. 'This is my source.'

He read it carefully, right through. It seemed to Kate to take several hours. At last he asked where she had got it.

'It was in the dressing chest, with the letters from Mrs Clifford,' she admitted in the most careless voice she could manage.

'And you didn't see fit to hand it to me?'

'I thought I had,' she lied. 'I was half-way to London when I found it in my bag and realized I'd forgotten about it. And it didn't then seem very important . . .'

'It was your duty to take it straight to the Yard, as you very well know, Mrs Theobald.'

'As a citizen,' she sighed, 'one has so many duties. As a newspaper reporter I have a few extra.'

Wake returned to the clipping, reading it through again, but quickly this time. Then he looked up at her. 'Suppose you now answer my question truthfully. Who told you?'

'Nobody,' she repeated. She explained how, searching newspaper files for contemporary reports of Captain Stallwood's court martial, they had stumbled on a picture of Tom Stevens, a con man in Malaya, who seemed very like Nicholas Bell; and how, delving back among the Tom Stevenses in the clippings library, she had winnowed the candidates to the youngster who had served a sentence for robbery. 'The dates sort of fitted, so we took a chance. I can't tell you what a relief it is to know we guessed right. Our lawyer said that, if we accidentally libelled a real and living Tom Stevens in Malaysia, it would cost £25,000.'

Leaning back, Wake allowed himself a grey little smile. 'I'm impressed, Mrs Theobald.'

'Henry thought you would be, and it's decent of you to admit it, after my behaviour. And now I'm going to come absolutely clean. I discovered by chance—or rather, Henry did—what connection that newspaper clipping had with Nicholas Bell, and everything that has happened. Henry was going to tell you immediately, but I nearly got gassed in my flat in London—you heard about that? Yes, I guess you would have. So Henry rushed up to London. He's a devoted husband, though I wouldn't much like him to hear me say so. And when I heard of it, I begged him to let me tell you. Because it's a terribly sad story. Captain Stallwood is Mamie Barrington's husband—there isn't really a Colonel Barrington. He's locked away as a hopeless lunatic, and she hasn't dared tell her son. Bell knew of it. He was in Malaya at the time, probably met her, or saw her, and recognized her back here in England. And he was blackmailing her about it, mostly for the pleasure of torturing her, she says. That's the background to the alcoholism. Major Sykes is in love with her, but she won't inflict herself on him.' She paused and stared at Wake. 'The suspicion is obvious, isn't it? But I tell you this. I'm not going to use even a hint of this story—unless, of course, it really was Major Sykes who killed Bell, and you arrest him. But I don't think it was, do you?'

'I know it wasn't,' replied Wake quietly.

Kate puffed out her cheeks. 'That's a relief. Now, there's some more information we've come across. Nicholas Bell's blue roses were stolen, and other plants substituted, some time before he was murdered.'

'In return, let me give you a hint, Mrs Theobald. You're on the wrong tack. You've already turned up, in your numerous and skilful enquiries, the one vital piece of information—if you could recognize it. And it has nothing to do with a rose.'

Kate regarded him questioningly.

157

'Also, I repeat my warning,' he went on. 'Don't try to investigate it on your own. That's what I'm here for, Mrs Theobald. It's for the police, not the newspapers.'

'What's the vital piece of information I've turned up?'

'Do you really expect me to go any further? All right, since you've become more co-operative. Just one small step further. Wasn't it Gertrude Stein who coined the famous remark, "A rose is a rose is a rose"?'

'I'll bet,' she told him with mock admiration, 'there isn't another officer in the Force with as much erudition as you.'

Wake permitted himself another thin smile. As he rose to show her out, he added, 'Let me adapt the quotation. "A crook is a crook is a crook."'

She drove back to Ashworth and parked outside the Nag's Head. On the way she had been trying to get Wake's meaning; and she thought she had.

Bob Ritchie was in the bar with a few others. Not to tip anybody off, she sent the girl in to fetch him out. He joined her in the car. 'Good to see you. Are you all right now?'

'Sure. And good to see you. Bob, I want some information quickly, and it's got to be dug out of the files.'

'Back in London? This nice weather?'

'Afraid so. What I got this morning was a hint that this whole thing is nothing to do with the village, but that it's about criminals. We know Nick Bell was one. And we know he's been living here in comfort for about 7 or 8 years. On what?'

'On the proceeds of something?'

'Obviously. So what we're looking for is a fairly substantial robbery, say between 6 and 9 years ago—he might have set himself up here as Nicholas Bell before he actually pulled the job, to have somewhere prepared to hide.'

'And it has to be a robbery for which the robbers weren't caught.'

'No, Bob. You disappoint me. Use your loaf. Bell was murdered.'

'I get it. He got away, but the other man—or men— didn't. So at last they catch up with him. How?'

'Heaven knows. Maybe they've only just got out.'

Ritchie doubted that. It would be one hell of a big robbery to earn sentences of 9 years or more, counting remission. More likely, he thought, that they had got out several years earlier and had been looking for him ever since—and suddenly found him.

Kate agreed. 'But we're not likely to spot it from this end of the period. It's the crime itself that ought to give us what we want. There were a good many at that time, of course, but there are several qualifying circumstances . . .'

'Sure. It's not too long a shot.'

'Ring me the moment you get it. If you can't reach me, leave a message where I can reach you.'

'Then can I come back?'

'Of course. If it's that kind of problem, I'll need you badly. Not a job for a woman, that.'

He slipped out of her car and went straight to his own, a small red Triumph sports, without going back into the pub for his things. So probably nobody would notice he had gone.

She watched him turn in the London direction, then drove herself to Mamie Barrington's bungalow. She understood now why the woman had lied to Henry. She must have been certain that it was Wilfred Sykes who had killed Bell, and she was trying to divert enquiries from him. So something could be relieved of the agony in which the wretched woman dwelled.

The village streets were empty; everybody indoors for

lunch. She hoped Mamie Barrington would be in, and not too far gone.

It was all right. She came to the door smelling strongly of gin, but still hard, cold, unfuddled. 'Your husband told you, then?'

'What else could he do?'

Mamie motioned to her to come in, offered her a drink, sat opposite her on the hard leather chairs when she refused. 'Well?'

'There could be only one reason for using that story,' Kate began. 'Maybe some muckrakers would use it anyway, but I'm not one of them. I'd not use a word of it unless something happened to force me. And that won't happen.' She paused. The look of anxiety, and the sudden touch of hope in the woman's eyes were almost too painful to bear. 'Major Sykes didn't kill Bell, and the police know that he didn't.'

Then the woman was weeping—silently, as though unable to sob aloud, but with tears oozing down her thin, tough cheeks. Kate wanted to get up and go to her, but knew that would be wrong.

'So there was no need to cook up some story to try to shield him,' said Kate briskly, as though nothing unusual were happening. 'Henry didn't believe you for a moment, anyway. He's a lawyer, remember, and quite skilled at detecting a lie—even a noble one. He doesn't think that Roger Wake believed you either, even at first. He's too good a policeman. Fortunately the question doesn't arise any more. But, as a matter of interest, did you invent it all, or did you really overhear a quarrel?'

She had stopped weeping. The tears were drying on her face, for she made no attempt to wipe them away.

'There was a quarrel, and of course I knew who it was—recognized the voice at once. But he didn't kill Bell. He went away soon after, out through the back entrance I suppose, and Bell came through into the cottage garden where I was waiting for him. He was laughing quietly to himself, in the evil sort of way he had. The quarrel had amused him. It had even put him in a good mood. He wasn't unpleasant to me that morning. He said there was no need to talk just yet, after all. We could meet again in a week or so. Meanwhile the cat permitted the mouse to scamper temporarily away—but without any illusions.'

'Who was the man quarrelling with Bell?'

'Dr Wisbech.'

After a pause, Kate said, 'You told Henry you didn't catch what they were rowing about. But, of course, you did.'

'It was about some roses. Bell was declaring that they had failed—I don't know why, or how. And I don't know why it was important. Bell was jeering at Dr Wisbech for being a poor botanist—no bloody good. The roses that had succeeded, he said, were those he had bred himself—nothing to do with Dr Wisbech. And Wisbech was shouting at him, raging in an awful temper. He was shouting that Bell wouldn't get away with it. He was shouting threats. He went off, shouting, and Bell came through into the cottage garden.'

'When you told Inspector Kippis, you concealed that you had seen Bell after the quarrel?'

Mamie nodded. 'I thought it must have been Wilfred who later . . . He was in such a fury when he found out what Bell was doing to me—a cold, silent fury. I know Wilfred so well.'

'Didn't you challenge him with it?'

'I didn't dare. I thought I knew already. So I thought that, if I could make the police believe that Bell had been killed by a man whose quarrel I overheard . . . Of course, I soon realized that it wouldn't work. But, by then, how could I go back on it?'

'You don't have to,' Kate reassured her. 'You deceived nobody. And now it no longer arises.'

As she got up, Mamie looked hard at the side table on which stood the bottles and glasses.

'Do you know,' she said, 'for the first time in years I believe I don't want a drink.'

Sir Gerald was not in his greenhouse or anywhere in the garden. Henry returned to ring the front-door bell. Rosa answered. He was upstairs in his den, working on his rose books. If it was really important, of course . . . She gazed sadly at the staircase. 'I seem to have been running up and down those stairs all day. Why don't you just go up? Second door on the right along the landing.'

At the old man's high-pitched, 'Who is it?' in response to Henry's knock, he opened the door and went in.

'Dear me, Mr Theobald, you do seem inclined to pop in on a fellow.'

'Lady Hawkes said to come straight up, if it was important. And it is. There's one question I ought to have asked you this morning. In fact, if I'd been a little more sensible, I should have asked you days ago. Did Nicholas Bell know you had taken his blue rose plants and substituted others with a similar leaf?'

'That's an extraordinary question, Mr Theobald. I think I resent it. In fact, I resent it rather strongly.'

'We've been to talk to Jack Clifford. He makes no secret that he was digging out Bell's blue roses at lunchtime on the day Bell was killed—when you saw Clifford through the door in the garden wall. It was by prior arrangement. Bell had asked him to take the rose plants to his nursery, to bud them on to as much stock as possible. Bell thought they were so precious that the job ought to be done by a professional. Clifford showed us the plants in his own garden this morning. They are in bloom—and they are not blue.'

'So many disappointments in this fascinating, maddening hobby,' said Sir Gerald with a delightful smile. 'Poor Bell. How upset he would have been to find his hoped-for blue rose turned out to be a failure after all. Or do you think he was trying to work up some sort of confidence trick, Mr Theobald? I see from your wife's intriguing account in today's paper that Bell was a man with a criminal record in which fraud figured prominently.'

'It won't wash, Sir Gerald. Clifford had seen one of the plants in bloom a couple of weeks earlier. Bell allowed one bloom to remain until he had seen it. It was pale blue. I daresay that Dr Wisbech had seen something of the kind too, although I haven't yet checked with him. And he's such a distinguished botanist that he will probably know several other points by which the plants could be identified. So may I please repeat my question? Did Nicholas Bell know?'

'I think I still resent the question.'

'Then there seems to be no alternative but to ask the police to put it to you. I think they'll want to, for otherwise a lot of suspicion might fall on Clifford.'

'Suspicion?'

'You yourself pointed out to me the possibility that murder could be committed for something as valuable as a blue rose. And Clifford's a professional rosarian who's thought to be in financial trouble.'

The ex-consul lifted his head and gave one of his shrill chuckles. 'Have no fear of that, Mr Theobald. The police have very good reason for not suspecting Jack Clifford of the murders—or me either, if you have that suspicion too. We both have, as it happens, a rather good alibi. On Monday morning, when Mrs Clifford was killed, Jack and I were in Linchester police station having a long talk with the Chief Superintendent. He asked me to call, because he wanted technical information about rose hybridization which might have a bearing on the case. I suggested taking Jack Clifford along too, since he is far more expert than I. We were still there when Dick Vernon, our village constable, phoned with the news that Mrs Clifford had been battered to death. Mr Wake himself broke it to Clifford. I've never seen a man crumble so badly. Pathetic, it was. Poor fellow. Pathetic.'

Accustomed to the witness who tries to dodge a straight question by proffering ample information about something else, Henry answered, 'I don't suppose anybody suspects either you or Jack Clifford of murder. But that wasn't my question. Did Bell know?'

The old man was no longer smiling. Without the smile, his face seemed grey and haggard. He was looking down at the rose books on his desk. He swallowed a couple of times, the adam's apple travelling prominently up and down his thin throat. Henry saw that he was ready to break. The point had not been far away. Good family, public school, university, the public service—always most honourable, truthful, respectable, respected; that was the man's life. And then in his seventies, infatuated by his roses, spurred by envy, he had committed his single crime. Henry pitied him. Challenged with something so alien to him, he was bound to break. All Henry had to do was softly to repeat the question : 'Did Bell know?'

With a slight shake of his head, he replied, 'No, he did not know. I substituted plants of my own a week before his death, when he was away in London for three days—long enough for the soil disturbance not to be noticed.' He tried a weak imitation of his charming smile. 'You see, Mr Theobald, I had thought out my crime carefully. But I made one mistake. Isn't it said that every criminal is betrayed by making one mistake? Mine was to show you one of the plants in bloom.'

'Why did you?'

'I thought it would strengthen my case if there were an independent witness to my blue rose before Clifford discovered that the plants in Bell's garden were not blue. What I didn't know was that Bell had asked Clifford to move the roses, and had shown him a bloom. I thought, when I saw him on that ill-fated Friday, that he was stealing Bell's roses, and so wouldn't dare to question mine.'

'Wisbech would have stumped you, though. He must have seen Bell's roses in bloom. He helped to breed them.'

Sir Gerald shook his head again. 'Bell was swindling him. Bell told him that the plant he had seen in bloom had faded back to lavender next day, and he had destroyed it. Dr Wisbech quarrelled violently with him, but there was nothing he could prove. He had no real claim to the rose, or any share of it. He couldn't even be certain that it had been a genuine blue rose at all.'

'How do you know that?'

'Dr Wisbech himself told me. He is a friend of mine. We are both on the committee of the local rose society. He was so angry that he blurted the whole thing out to me. There was no danger to me from that quarter.'

They sat in silence. The motive, Henry felt sure, had not been the value of the rose. The old man cared little for money. It was an obsession that, fed by envy, had grown into a crime.

At last Sir Gerald asked in a low voice, 'What do I have to do? Go to the police?'

Henry considered. But nothing would be gained, except the wreck of an old man's life. 'I think it would be enough,' he suggested, 'if you put the plants back in Bell's paddock, in the position from which you took them.'

A look of pain came on to the old man's face. 'I have told my closest friend, a national expert, that I have such a rose. I have boasted of it, my dear young man. I have promised to send it for trials, and have declared that I will name it after my wife. A blue rose called Rosa Hawkes! It would have crowned our marriage.'

'It isn't your rose,' Henry gently reminded him.

'But who wants it now? Bell is dead.'

'It could be, you say, worth £100,000. It is part of his estate—the major part, probably. He may have relatives, I don't know. It may be possible to show that his rose establishment was financed from a crime, so that the people he robbed or defrauded might have some claim on the proceeds; or, more probably, they would go to the Crown.'

'Be damned to the money. I'll make it over to any charity you name.'

'The roses must be returned.'

'But what shall I tell my friend, or my wife?'

'To your friend, some excuse you will manufacture. To Lady Hawkes, I suggest, the truth.'

Stella Sims was at the Old Rectory, full of solicitude for Kate, insisting on carving up cold meats from the fridge and tossing a salad for the two of them, late in the afternoon though it was. Stella was even brighter and gayer than ever; a forced gaiety, Henry thought. There were marks of anxiety under her eyes, and a couple of times she seemed to drop into a daydream, rousing herself with a start, laughing and making some joking remark.

Jonathan brought Anne Brodie back from the university for tea and they stayed for drinks and supper. It was only after that, when Jonathan and the two women drove off at about 8 o'clock for a dance in Linchester, that Kate and Henry could settle to exchange news of their day.

How sad, sighed Kate, that she could not use the story of the switched roses.

'But you can't,' cried Henry alarmed.

'No dear, of course I can't. All other considerations aside, the lawyer wouldn't pass it for the paper. Just as I can't use anything I got from Mamie. What a pity! They're both wonderful stories.'

Henry said he did not set much store by what Mamie had told her. So far as he could see, it disproved nothing that mattered. 'And what's more,' he said, 'Wake didn't deny anything that matters, either.'

'Perhaps I'm a bit tired sweetheart, but I'm not with you.'

'Wake said it wasn't Wilfred Sykes who killed Bell. But that's all he said. You, out of pity for the woman, went round to pass this on to Mamie, who spent a long time convincing you of her relief, because she had desperately feared that it had been Sykes who killed Bell for her sake—or so she said.'

Kate was puzzled. 'Why shouldn't we believe her? The fear was genuine enough. If you had seen the look in her eyes when I told her what Wake had said, you'd have had no doubt of it. And she was actually weeping. I'll swear she thought her lover had killed Bell. I'm sure of it. At the end, she didn't even want a drink.'

Henry smiled. 'The last bit's the most convincing. I don't necessarily buy any of the rest. Suppose Mamie had invented all that stuff about overhearing a quarrel, simply to cover up her real reason for being at Howth Lodge that morning. Isn't that more probable? I never believed in that overheard quarrel in the first place, and you've told me nothing that makes me change my view.'

'Which is?'

'What I said before. Mamie killed Bell in a rage that morning, and Sykes killed Sally Clifford in a panic when he was disturbed on Monday morning in the cottage, and then knocked you out. Did Wake say anything that would refute that idea?'

'In a sense, yes. He hinted strongly that the whole

thing is to do with a crime—some old crime, I reckon. Major Sykes and Mamie have nothing to do with that.'

'How do we know?' demanded Henry. 'They were all out in Malaya when Stevens, alias Bell, organized a large-scale fraud. How do we know they weren't all mixed up in that?'

'Wild speculation, Theobald. I'm shocked at you, with your legal training and all.'

'No, but seriously,' he continued, 'who else is there? Clifford and Sir Gerald are eliminated from the list, even if they were ever seriously on it. We long ago agreed that Billy Tooth is a non-starter. There's Jonathan, of course. You can't have failed to notice how anxious Stella still is. But the point his girl-friend made seems to me conclusive. I could imagine him killing Bell in a rage at what had happened to Anne Brodie. But I can't conceive him, in any circumstances, battering Sally Clifford's head in—or imagine any reason why he should. So, aside from Wilfred Sykes and Mamie, who else is there?'

'Dr Wisbech.'

Henry snorted. 'That makes me sure that Mamie invented the overheard quarrel. Every time Wisbech's name is dragged in, it turns out to be a red herring. And even suppose she really did hear the quarrel and recognize Wisbech's voice, that still doesn't nail him. Mamie herself went on to say that Wisbech made off, and she saw Bell a few minutes later. If the quarrel is to be taken as true, then so must the sequel. Either way, true or false, Wisbech isn't implicated. So it simply has to be Sykes and Mamie. There's nobody else in the whole group— with a slight hesitation about Jonathan.'

The phone rang. He went into the hall to answer it and called that it was for her—Bob Ritchie.

She came back flushed with the news.

'It doesn't have to be anyone in the group at all. I tried

to follow up the hint that Roger Wake gave me. A crook is a crook is a crook, he said, and that was the vital piece of information. So I sent Bob searching through the files for a big robbery that fitted, about 6 to 9 years ago, and he's found it. There's only one that fits, Bob says. Seven years ago, 3 men snatched £87,000 in notes in a bank raid in Lancashire. Two were caught and sentenced to 7 years each—which means they got out about 2 years ago, perhaps a bit earlier. The third was never caught or named. The others didn't give him away. But in the police statement there was evidence that one of them had threatened to find the third one day, and do him.'

'So the one who got away was Bell, you reckon?'

'I think it's what Roger Wake was hinting.'

'Why should he hint it to you?' mused Henry. 'It could only be because he hoped you'd follow it up and publicize it. So he wants you to, Kate.'

'Bob will be here in the morning with pictures of the 2 men who were sentenced,' she said. 'He's getting them from some police source. Bob has friends at the Yard, I believe. Freddie Henderson and Jim Tapp are the villains' names. And right villains too, says Bob. Criminal records as long as your walking stick, and very violent gents, particularly Jim Tapp. I can't use the names, of course, or identify the actual bank raid—it wouldn't be safe yet. I'll have to get Wake to confirm it.'

'You ought to tell him now.'

'He can read it all in the *Post* tomorrow morning, sweetheart. Slayings not for roses after all. Bank robbers' vengeance. Desperate criminals spend years tracking down the man who shopped them—and strike home. Great stuff, darling.'

'If Wake put you on to it,' Henry was still objecting, 'it's because he's using you again. Watch it, Kate. Check with him first. It can't be as simple as it sounds.'

'Let him do his own detecting. And don't stand between a girl with an exclusive and her typewriter, my love. Shove over—and shut up for half an hour till I've done my thing.'

Henry picked up a book from a side table and tried to read while Kate tapped away. But his thoughts were too uneasy. If it were that sort of danger, Wake had no right to put her into it. Next morning, Henry decided to himself, he'd have a quiet word with the Chief Superintendent and demand to know what the hell he was doing.

CHAPTER XV

HENRY TOOK THE CAR in the morning to drive into Linchester; Kate wouldn't want it because Bob Ritchie would soon be back from London, and he could drive her. What did Henry want to go into Linchester for, anyway? Oh, just one or two ideas he'd like to try out, he told her. Kate enquired no further. She and Henry did not pry into each other; never had.

Scarcely had he gone, leaving Kate to finish her coffee at the breakfast table—Jonathan and Stella were unlikely to be down for an hour or more, seeing it was Saturday —when Dereck Andrews drove up. 'What's all this marvellous stuff you've got in the *Post* this morning, Kate? What's the strength of it?'

'A little guesswork,' she admitted, 'but basically sound.'

Dereck mused that, in a way, it was a pity. Vengeful criminals were all very well, but not to be compared to murders for a blue rose.

'Well, that's the way it is,' she told him. 'And in one way I'm not sorry. I've got quite fond of the people around here.'

'Talking of people around here, most of them this morning seem to be policemen. On the way I saw 3 carloads, not seeming to be going anywhere much. And there's a couple of plain-clothes men on foot lurking about in your shrubbery.'

'So,' murmured Kate thoughtfully.

He asked for a tip to give him a start for his piece for Sunday. But Kate shook her head. What she had, she reckoned she could hold for Monday morning's paper. 'Sorry, Dereck. But I think it's all going to break quite soon now.'

Not long after he had gone, Bob Ritchie telephoned. He was at the Nag's Head. What did she want him to do?

'Listen, Bob, Roger Wake has put some sort of police guard round me, and I want to duck it. I've got a marvellous hunch for Monday's piece, but it won't help to have coppers skulking around while we try it. So you've got to get me away on the quiet. There's a back gate at the far end of the Old Rectory garden, by a humpback bridge over a little stream. You've seen it? Good. Be there in half an hour. Bring a car rug, or something I can duck under if need be.'

'If Wake thinks you should have police protection, maybe it's not such a good idea to dodge it,' he uneasily objected.

'But I shall have a brawny Scots newspaper reporter to protect me,' she replied sweetly. 'You be there in half an hour, friend, and we'll argue the toss later.'

The sun was bright, the morning heating up. She put on her sunbathing dress and big dark glasses, picked up a couple of magazines and a little radio from the living-room and a deckchair from the porch, and wandered off into the garden. She could not spot the plain-clothes men behind the shrubs but had no doubt they had seen her. She crossed the lawn behind the Old Rectory and picked a shelter behind a vast rhododendron. The garden beyond had been let go into wilderness. The Simses were not gardening people, except for a terrace for drinks.

She raised the canopy of her chair and turned its back to the house. She stretched out in the sun, turned on the radio loud and flipped open a magazine. She gave them 15 minutes. By then, she reckoned, they'd have scouted round to see where she was, and returned to their post out front where they'd be within reach of a radio car. Then she slipped quickly round the rhododendron on to what remained of a path through the wilderness. The back gate, she was glad to find, was not locked. Bob was sitting on the rail of the humpback bridge, lazily contemplating the stream. When she emerged, he got up and wandered out of sight. She waited. In a couple of minutes his little red sports car came slowly along the lane, stopping just long enough for her to nip in.

'To the back gate to Howth Lodge,' she instructed, sitting as low as she could in the seat, sheltering beneath the car rug.

'You'll find the pictures on the dashboard shelf.'

She groped for them. Jim Tapp was a short, rat-faced man with dark greasy hair; Freddie Henderson taller, red-headed, with a loose mouth, thin nose, querulous expression.

'What's the marvellous idea?' asked Bob.

'That bank raid in Lancashire—was the money recovered?'

'Not a penny. You mean, if Bell was the thief they didn't catch, chances are he had the money, or what was left of it, stowed away somewhere.'

'Must have,' reasoned Kate. 'What else would Henderson and Tapp have been looking for when they more or less tore the cottage to pieces, the morning that poor Sally Clifford interrupted them, and then Henry and I?

'The sequence seems fairly obvious now. Bell, Henderson and Tapp made the bank raid. Bell double-crossed the others somehow and probably shopped them. He had already established himself in this village as an amiable retired businessman from the Far East—unbeknownst, of course, to his chums Henderson and Tapp. So he returns quietly to Howth Lodge with the stolen notes and lives in comfort and idleness, devoting himself to his two hobbies.

'Henderson and Tapp, having gone down for the raid, get out of gaol about 2½ years ago and start looking for him. At last they locate him—how, I simply don't know. Friday of last week they catch up with him, stab him in the throat with some gardening tool of his own—and take it away, I suppose in case of fingerprints. Something must have prevented them from searching the cottage straight away. So they hang about, wait until the police have locked the place up and gone away, and 3 days later break in through the back and start to tear the walls down, looking for the dough.'

'Suppose he'd put it in a bank.'

'He would scarcely have done that,' she reasoned. 'No doubt he got some in—enough to account for modest day-to-day living. If he'd tried to get a lot of used banknotes in, except in driblets, he'd surely have aroused suspicion. Anyway, why should he bank it? Banks tell on you to the income-tax men. He probably bought a few securities—just enough to satisfy them that he was living on a small investment income. And kept the rest in the house somewhere, to take out as and when needed.'

'So we try to find it,' said Bob. 'And if we do?'

'Then we break the story in Monday's paper—having reported the find to Roger Wake very late on Sunday night.'

'Just one snag occurs to me,' he then remarked. 'Why do you suppose we may be able to find the money when Henderson and Tapp tore the place down and failed?'

'Feminine intuition. Think, Bob. If it isn't in the house . . .'

'Then it's in the greenhouse. Right?'

'Right.'

She showed him where the barbed wire had been snipped away from the top of the fence and boxes placed to make it easy to get over. 'Mind that rusty nail. Last time, I tore my skirt on it twice.'

'Dress you've got on now,' he said, 'there isn't all that much to worry about.'

The greenhouse door was locked. Bob pulled out a thin pocket-knife, fumbled with it for a couple of minutes and released the latch. 'Not much of a lock, if it's a treasure house.'

'No point in having a good lock,' replied Kate. 'Anybody could cut through a pane of glass and get in. A good lock might even have aroused suspicion—if anyone ever suspected anything.'

The heat inside was intense. The plants had all withered for want of water. 'Seems a shame,' said Bob, 'when the water's actually here.' He pointed to a large zinc water tank at the far end, fed with rain water by pipes from the gutters outside.

'Here was where his body was,' murmured Kate, feeling even a little queasy at the recollection. 'You can still see the marks of blood on the bench there, and the wooden slats of the floor.' She was gazing at the bench. The knives with which he had been working were still scattered there, starting to rust slightly from condensation. The pots of roses, withered and leafless now, still lay where he had knocked them as he fell. 'Ugh! Let's get on with it,' she said.

Bob was already looking carefully round. The only possibilities, he pointed out, were beneath the floor or in the brick wall against which the greenhouse leaned.

He tried the floor first. He eased up the slats in sections to probe the soil beneath with a garden fork that hung by the door. Although the ground was hard, he exerted all his strength and sank the tines to their full length at each point. If it were buried under the floor, he told her, it must be at a greater depth than the fork could pierce, which didn't seem likely, for how could Bell have got at it?

Next he tried the brick wall, tracing his fingers along every line of mortar, seeking the hint of an opening. It took him more than half an hour to traverse the whole length of the wall inside the greenhouse. At the end he rose, soaked in sweat. 'Nothing there that I can find. You guessed wrong, Kate.'

'It must be here,' she insisted. 'If it had been in the cottage, they'd have found it when they tore the place apart, or the police would have found it afterwards. You can bet Roger Wake had every brick in that building probed, trying to find whatever it was the intruders were looking for. So it can't be in the house. So it must be here.'

Bob made a comic face. 'What's that? Feminine logic? It could be anywhere—or nowhere. We could be wrong. Maybe Bell wasn't involved in the bank raid. Maybe there weren't any vengeful hoods gunning for him.'

'Bob dear,' she said irritably, 'please don't make difficulties. Just think.'

He scratched his head. 'Okay. Let's try to imagine we're Bell, 7 or 8 years ago. He has got to make a hidden place for a considerable volume of notes. What has he got to help him?' He looked slowly round. 'Electricity. That's a tool.'

He stepped to the electricity switchboard at the entrance end of the greenhouse. 'Now then, I used to know a bit about electricity. These are the switches for the heating system, linked to the time clock. And these . . .'

He switched them on. 'Ah, these are for the extractor fans. This lot must control the humidifying system. If the police had switched them on, the roses would be as good as ever. It's fed from the rainwater tank. And there's one more switch.' He switched it on. Nothing happened.

'Perhaps it's a spare,' suggested Kate.

Bob was feeling with his fingers behind the panel. 'There's a wire,' he murmured. 'Look, it runs along the back edge of the bench as far as this socket, with a 13-amp plug to carry it on. Hey, wait a minute.' He was searching among the small tools on the upper shelves to find a screwdriver. Then he quickly unfastened the plug.

'Clever, ain't it? It's a fused plug—and there's no fuse. So if anybody accidentally presses that switch, nothing happens. When Bell wanted something to happen, he unscrewed the plug, slipped in a little fuse tube, and there it was.'

'Where do we get a little fuse tube?'

He was already unscrewing a plug from the heating circuit. He whipped out the fuse, inserted it in the bench plug, shoved it back in the socket, and Kate depressed the switch on the panel.

Slowly and soundlessly the huge zinc water-tank pivoted on its fronthand left corner.

'A little 5 horse-power motor somewhere,' muttered Bob, 'and the tank running on hidden ballbearings. Couldn't be simpler, really. Try the switch the other way, Kate.'

The tank slowly moved back into place.

She depressed the switch again, moved the tank out, and they both peered into the large concreted cavity beneath where it stood. The cavity contained a number of aluminium boxes, all except the nearest carefully sealed against atmosphere.

'He'd even put in a small electric heater to deal with

condensation which might have caused mildew,' murmured Bob. 'You have to admire him.'

Kate opened the nearest box. It was half full of packets of used £1 notes, each in a rubber band. On top lay a small black leather notebook.

'This was his bankbook,' said Bob, studying it. 'Every time he drew on the store, he noted the amount and the date. In 7 years he had drawn just over £33,000—tax free! And that leaves nearly £54,000 still in this hole.'

'Just back up to the end and don't make a noise.'

At the sound of the sharp, harsh voice they both pivoted. Two men stood in the doorway of the greenhouse, the tall sandy-haired one behind, and in front the short, sallow-faced, greasy-haired one in a worn dark-blue suit; and in his hand a nasty-looking revolver.

CHAPTER XVI

At Linchester police station Henry was shown into Roger Wake's office directly he asked for him.

Wake looked up from a dossier he was studying, one hand clutched into his hair. He reached across his desk to pull out from a pile of papers the clip of Kate's *Post* story that morning. 'Your wife took something of a chance, Mr Theobald.'

Henry regarded him steadily. 'Aren't you taking something of a chance too, Mr Wake?'

Wake nodded hesitantly, as though to concede that he supposed you could call it that. It was correct, as Mrs Theobald had stated in the *Post* that morning, that the police were seeking two criminals who had served long sentences for a major robbery, who they thought could help them in their enquiries into the murders at Howth Lodge. It was true that the police believed that Nicholas

Bell, whose real name was Thomas Stevens, and who had a criminal record, was linked in the past with the 2 men the police wished to interview. 'There are embellishments in your wife's story which are not quite accurate. But, by and large, she has got it right.'

'Would she also have been right if she had printed the men's names—James Tapp and Frederick Henderson?'

The Chief Superintendent eased himself lazily back in his seat. 'I see we must try to recruit Mrs Theobald. The newspaper files again?'

'Yes. There was only one major robbery that really fitted. You applied much the same sort of reasoning, no doubt.'

Wake permitted himself a tremor of a smile. 'Something of the kind—except that we used our own records rather than those in a newspaper library. We also had something rather more substantial to go on. Henderson was seen in Linchester the day after Nicholas Bell was murdered, by a police officer serving here who happened to have served in the London borough in which Henderson lived some years ago. Unfortunately this officer was not aware that we had just put a pin on Henderson and Tapp as the likely men, and wanted them. Had it been a few hours later, he would have been brought in— and Mrs Clifford would probably be alive and your wife would not have been attacked. Yes, of course we think they were looking for what remains of the stolen money. We are also fairly sure that they were up the wrong tree and it isn't at Howth Lodge. Though where Bell cached it is something of a puzzle. He worked a certain amount into bank accounts over the years, and invested some in small sums in unit trusts and such. But it was a mere fraction of the total.'

Henry asked, 'Do you know where Henderson is now?'

'No. He and Tapp were both last known to have been in a Soho club on the night on which they attempted to kill your wife by filling your flat with gas. Oh yes, there's not much doubt of that. She was a little rash in hinting, in the *Post*, that she had seen her assailant and might recognize him again.'

'She hadn't. That story was written for her by a friend while she was still under sedation. I gave him all the facts I could but not that one, which isn't true anyway. I suppose he felt at liberty to embroider a bit.'

'A pity he chose that particular piece of embroidery. But in one sense she had a lucky escape. If they had known what would appear in the *Post* next morning —the actual identity of Tom Stevens—I'm pretty sure they'd have killed her as she lay in bed, without trying for the illusion of an accident. If Mrs Theobald intends to continue her career as a sensational crime reporter, I advise you to take your name and address out of the telephone directory, put stronger locks on your doors, and don't leave her alone at night.'

Henry, who had kept his temper so far, now broke out at the fellow's insufferable, rather mocking calm.

'What it amounts to is that you gave my wife enough of a hint to produce the story that in fact she published this morning—in the hope that she would then attract Henderson and Tapp, whom you've lost. Isn't that it? If you let her run into any danger, Wake, I promise you a scandal that will run right through the police, let alone what it will do to you personally.'

Wake raised his hand gently to check him. 'It was Mrs Theobald who, disregarding my strong and repeated warnings, blundered against these men by trying to carry out a newspaper investigation independently of the police. The responsibility is not ours. Address yourself to her editor, who allows a young woman to take such risks. But you need have no anxiety, Mr Theobald. Of course I see your point. And I assure you that there's a mobile police guard round your wife that I don't think any known criminals could pierce. She's perfectly safe, Mr Theobald.'

Before he left Linchester, Henry telephoned Sir Gerald. 'Have you made up your mind about the roses?'

'Yes, Mr Theobald. I have been thinking about the matter all night, without sleeping. And you're quite right. I have behaved dishonourably. Worse, I am a thief. The roses are not mine and I must not try to claim them.'

His voice was subdued, weary. There was none of the high-pitched cackle in it. Henry felt deeply sorry for the old man. But to relent would be pointless—indeed, impossible.

'Will you do it this morning, Sir Gerald? Good. I should like somebody to be there, so that there can be no doubt that the roses have been returned. Clearly, it must be an expert. Would you object if I brought Jack Clifford along as witness?'

'Not at all,' came the old man's voice hesitantly, 'if, that is, he is willing.'

'He'll come,' promised Henry. 'Shall we say 11 o'clock?'

'Any time you wish.'

'Eleven then, in the paddock at Howth Lodge. We'll have to go over the back fence, unless you want me to bring the police into it—and I don't suppose you do.'

'Not unless you feel it is essential, Mr Theobald.' He sounded resigned, beaten. 'I shall raise no objection, whatever you see fit to do.'

'I don't think there's any need to bring in the police —not at this stage, anyhow. It seems the murders were committed by former criminal associates of Bell. Nothing to do with roses. If that matter is put right, and the roses quietly returned to where they came from, I see no reason for saying any more about it. Eleven o'clock then, Sir Gerald.'

Henry drove straight to Clifford's Rose Nurseries. He asked for Mr Clifford at the office and was directed to the house. Jack Clifford himself came to the door. He was dressed and shaved. Perhaps, thought Henry, his acute despair was passing and there was hope for him. Then the man himself supplied the reason. Betty, his daughter, was out of the clinic and coming home that afternoon. She was all right. He was thinking of today, he said, as the end of a chapter.

'There's just one more thing to be cleared up before the chapter closes, and I want your help,' said Henry. He told him about Sir Gerald.

Clifford looked incredulous. 'Sir Gerald took them? I'd never have believed it.'

'Out of character, certainly. I think it's only now that he realizes fully what he has done. When I spoke to him on the phone this morning he sounded like a man who had just woken up from a dream—or perhaps a nightmare. Anyhow, he has undertaken to replace the roses in Howth Lodge paddock at 11 o'clock this morning. I said I wanted an expert there as witness and suggested you. It needs somebody who can identify plants, if none of them happens to be in bloom—and in case there's any more nonsense. Is it possible to mark them in any way?'

'Not with certainty. But I'll bring a camera with a close-up lens and photograph each plant from all sides once Sir Gerald has put them back. You can take the film and have it developed—and hold the negatives until it's decided what's to become of the plants. What will happen, do you reckon?'

Henry said he didn't know. He thought Bell had probably died intestate, and doubted whether, even if relatives could be traced, they would be permitted to inherit what could be counted the proceeds of crime. The Crown would probably get them in the end.

'Do you think I could buy them, at a reasonable figure? I'd be taking a big risk.'

'Probably. But you'll have to wait until everything is sorted out.'

Clifford fetched his camera. They set off towards the village.

'We've time to call at the Old Rectory first and pick up my wife,' said Henry. 'She'd never forgive me if she wasn't in on this.'

'She'll not write about it?' asked Clifford nervously.

'Not unless it becomes part of the case. And obviously it won't.'

At the Old Rectory they looked into the living-room. Jonathan was deep in a chair by the window, books spread open all round him.

'Kate? She's gone out somewhere. She was in the garden, but she's not there now. She left the radio switched on, so I went down to ask her to turn it off. But she'd gone.'

Henry felt fear rising within him. He went to the phone, called the Nag's Head. 'Hallo. Who's that? Oh, Dereck, I'm glad it's you. Is Bob Ritchie there? Went where? To pick up Kate? Oh, thanks. Yes, that's a relief. I didn't know where she'd gone. But if Bob's with her . . .'

He went back to Jonathan. 'Bob's with her—another reporter from the *Post*. All the same, I think I'll go and look for her, once we've finished the rose replanting.'

'Rose replanting?'

Henry told him briefly what was on, being a little vague about what Sir Gerald had actually done. Jonathan asked if he could come too.

'A completely impartial witness might be a good idea,'

agreed Henry. 'Jack Clifford's outside in my car. No need to take yours.'

At the corner of the lane, where it turned towards the rear of Howth Lodge paddock, Henry braked suddenly. Two cars stood in the lane by the gate, which was now open. The front car he recognized as Bob Ritchie's little red sports. The other was a large old Humber.

He suddenly felt premonition, a prickle of fear at the nape of his neck. On impulse, he backed his own car out of sight.

'May be silly,' he told them, 'but I've got an uneasy feeling. Kate and Bob must be in there—it's his red sports car. I want to find out what the other is, without giving warning.'

Jonathan nodded and stepped out with him. They peered round the corner. A tall, sandy-haired man was stowing a metal box in the boot of the Humber.

Jonathan gently took Henry's arm and drew him back out of sight. 'That chap was in the garden of Howth Lodge the morning Sally Clifford was killed. You came out of the kitchen, but he hid behind some bushes. When you went in again, he scrambled over the wall.'

'You were there?'

'Yes, can't tell you about it now. Later.'

Henry hurriedly backed the car to a nearby gate where he could turn. 'Mr Clifford, you take the car. Get back into the village and find the police. There's a mobile patrol around. Bring them here as quick as you can, but tell them to close in without giving themselves away. Kate's in there. Jon and I are going to get her out.'

Clifford nodded, said nothing, slid into the driver's seat, moved off as quietly as he could.

Jonathan, at the corner, gestured to Henry. 'He's gone back in again, and left the gate open. He must be bringing a load out into the car. If we're quick . . .'

183

They moved as fast as they could down the lane. Peering round the gate entrance, Jonathan reported, 'He's coming back with another case. Coming out of the greenhouse. There are people in there—can't see who.'

Henry glanced round desperately. From the toolbag in the open boot of the Humber he picked out a couple of heavy wrenches, passing one to Jonathan. They flattened themselves against the fence to the near side of the gate, not daring to risk crossing the gap.

As the man drew near they could hear him panting. He was in a hurry. He came through the gate, clutching the case, not looking to either side.

Henry got him with one crack on the back of his head. He dropped without a shout; only the clatter of the metal box falling. Jonathan was already standing over him while Henry pulled out his shoelaces, knotting them together, then bound his wrists behind his back. Jonathan found a length of rope in Bob Ritchie's car. They fastened it tightly round the man's legs. He was moaning now. From the Humber boot Henry took an oily rag and, forcing the man's jaws, stuffed it into his mouth, tying another strip round his head. He knew the fastenings wouldn't last long if the man regained consciousness. But they should not have to last long. Clifford must soon be back with the police.

He motioned to Jonathan. Picking up the wrenches, they went swiftly through the gateway, moving fast towards the greenhouse. Luckily the path between the rose beds was grassed.

Then Henry checked, aghast. He could see into the greenhouse now. Kate and Bob Ritchie were standing flat against a big tank which seemed to have been moved into the far end. Facing them was a small, black-haired man. In his fist Henry could see the little revolver.

The man had his back to the pathway.

Henry moved in as swiftly as he dared. Kate and Bob

must have seen him. They had enough sense not to show it.

He'd have to chance it. Drawing back his arm, he pitched his wrench at the greenhouse.

The pane it hit shattered with a crash. The man swung viciously round.

Bob took him with a horizontal rugger tackle, crushing him against the end of the greenhouse, striking his head on the jamb of the door, fracturing more glass with his shoulder. The gun flew out on to the path. Jonathan grabbed it, helped Bob get the man up.

Henry ran past them to take Kate in his arms. She was sobbing.

'Okay now, darling.'

She held back her sobs, clutching his shoulders. 'Okay now.'

The first police were coming in fast through the back gate. At the same time the door in the garden wall opened and more ran in that way.

CHAPTER XVII

FROM THE POLICE STAFF CAR that drew up outside Howth Lodge came Detective Chief Superintendent Roger Wake, followed by Detective-Inspector Kippis, hurrying through the garden, almost running.

With his arm round Kate, Henry greeted him: 'Perfectly safe, eh, Wake?'

Kate freed herself. 'It was my fault. I knew there was a police guard, and I ducked it. I'm sorry, Mr Wake.'

'Do you feel up to telling us what happened—or must we wait until we read it in your newspaper?' he asked, smiling almost broadly for him.

'I reckoned that the money couldn't be in the house,

for you'd have searched it thoroughly. So I thought it might be in the greenhouse. It would make a good story to find it. So I got Bob to pick me up at the back gate of the Simses' house, and we came here.

'After we'd searched round for awhile, Bob reckoned that either the money wasn't there, or there must be some gimmick, some gadget. So he tried the electric panel—and hit on the way to move the water tank.

'We'd just got it open when Tapp—I suppose it's Tapp and Henderson—held us up with a gun from the door. Henderson was behind him.

'Bob made one damn good effort. When Henderson got within reach, to start lifting out the boxes of notes, Bob grabbed him and tried to shove him in front of me.'

'But Tapp was too quick for me,' said Ritchie. 'He got hold of Kate and held the gun to her head. So I had to let the other bastard go. Then Tapp backed us up against the tank while Henderson lugged out the boxes from the cavity beneath and went off with them, one by one. I don't know where.'

'Stacking them in a car in the lane,' Henry told him.

'They were working as fast as they could,' Kate took up. 'Tapp was growling with temper after Bob made that grab at Henderson. He took pleasure in telling us what was going to happen to us.'

'Which was?'

'Shoot us,' said Bob, 'and put us in the cavity beneath the tank. Nobody would find us there, he said. Henderson would drive my car away and tumble it over a cliff into the sea. By the time the police had sorted that out, he and Henderson would be well clear and lying low in some other country.'

Henry turned to Wake. 'If you want additional evidence against Henderson, Jonathan Sims has it. He saw him in the garden of Howth Lodge the morning Sally Clifford was killed, when Kate and I arrived at the cottage. By the way, Jonathan, what were you doing there? You said you'd tell me later.'

Jonathan Sims looked at the Chief Superintendent. 'There's something I have to tell you.'

'I know what it is, sir,' replied Wake. 'You're going to tell me that when you came to Howth Lodge at 2.30 in the afternoon, you found Nicholas Bell's body in the greenhouse. He was already dead.'

Jonathan was pale. 'You knew?'

'He must have been dead already.'

'I think he'd been dead for some little time,' said Jonathan. 'The blood was congealing.'

'Why didn't you report it to us at once, sir?'

'The night before, Anne Brodie had broken down and told me what had happened between her and Nick Bell. I went round to tell him to get out of this place. If he'd been alive, I think I might have killed him. When I found him dead, I thought Anne had.'

'Why did you think that, sir?'

'She had reason for it. And I thought it must have been a woman, because there was a small pearl earring on the floor of the greenhouse near where he had fallen. It was stained with some of his blood. I picked it up and took it away. I hesitated for hours, what to do. I dared not ask Anne herself. I simply dared not. And when some hours had passed, I realized I couldn't go to the police without explaining the delay.'

'You were pretty cool when you took us up there for drinks that evening,' murmured Kate.

'I was desperate. The body had to be found, and I had to be there to control it. I took you into the garden deliberately . . .'

'That was sweet of you.'

Henry asked, 'Why did you come back on the Monday morning, when Sally Clifford was killed?'

'In case the other earring had been dropped too. I

thought of that possibility too late to do anything about it until the police had gone. While I was searching the greenhouse—the door was easy to unlock—I heard a sound in the cottage garden. Then I saw that a ladder had been put against the wall. I climbed it and saw this man Henderson running for some bushes on the far side. Henry came dashing out of the cottage, but by then the man was hidden. Henry went back in. Henderson scrambled over the wall. The noise must have alerted Henry again. He came out, went to the bushes where the man had hidden, and later went back into the cottage. I reckoned I'd better scram. I don't know any more.'

'An earring,' mused Kate. 'Wasn't there somebody else looking for an earring? Why yes, when we went to get the key from the old charwoman that morning, she said Sally Clifford had borrowed it because she thought she had dropped an earring there . . .'

They all turned slowly to look at Jack Clifford.

'Sally Clifford . . .' repeated Kate softly.

Jack Clifford gazed miserably at the Superintendent. 'I suppose you know.'

'Put it this way, sir,' Wake replied. 'I know that Bell wasn't killed by Tapp or Henderson. We've checked on their movements, as far as we could. That day they were in a Soho club most of the time. They had no idea where Tom Stevens was, I'm sure—until Mrs Theobald published the photograph of Nicholas Bell in the *Post*, the morning after he was murdered. That brought them here fast. But we missed them.'

'The night before, Betty told her mother she was pregnant. She was only fifteen. She wouldn't say who the man was. Sally was distraught. She adored the child. So do I.'

He paused, silent, as though there were nothing more to say.

'And then, sir?'

'Next morning I went down to the office at the Nursery

to phone my sister in Wimbledon, to arrange for Betty to go to stay with her, and then we'd get her into an abortion clinic. Perhaps we could keep it quiet after all. When I got back to the house, Betty was alone. She was crying bitterly. I drove her to the station and put her on the train to London. She'd calmed down a bit by then. I still hadn't realized what had happened . . .'

Again he stopped, silent, as though in a coma. Nobody spoke that time. After a long interval, he went on : 'When I got back to the house, Sally came in, almost demented. It took a while for me to get any sense out of her. Then she told me. While I was out, Betty had confessed. The man was Nick Bell. Sally almost went mad. As you know from those letters, Mr Wake, my wife had had an affair with Bell, but it had stopped several months ago, and it was at an end, forgiven. Then to find that he had seduced our daughter . . .'

The man was weeping silently now. His face was wet with weeping. Kate, herself almost crying, begged, 'Stop him, please. Stop him.'

'You don't have to say anything, Mr Clifford,' interrupted Henry. 'I'm speaking as a lawyer. I advise you not to say anything.'

'Mr Theobald is quite right,' agreed Wake. 'You need say nothing more, Mr Clifford. But I must caution you that, if you wish to say any more, what you say will be taken down by this police officer here, and may be used in evidence against you.'

Clifford waved the objections aside. 'Do you think I care? I have to tell you. I can't go on, without speaking of it. Sally ran out to the stable to get her horse. She'd been used to riding over to Bell's place, by back ways, through the woods. She found him in the greenhouse, challenged him with it. He didn't attempt to deny it. Instead, he started to tell her the differences between the ways she and her daughter had reacted in bed. He told her Betty enjoyed being whipped . . . And some of the other things he had done to her . . .'

Kate moved impulsively, to go to him, but Henry took her arm and held her still.

'She had a grass shears in her pocket, and she stabbed him in the neck. When he fell, she ran away in horror, rode home wildly, and I found her, rambling almost as though she'd gone mad. When at last I got it out of of her, I realized she'd be traced at once through the shears.'

Henry interrupted quickly. 'Don't say any more, Mr Clifford, until you have taken counsel with your lawyer.'

'That's sound advice, Mr Clifford,' said Wake.

But Clifford waved them aside again. 'If you charge me, I plead guilty. I got into the Land-Rover, drove there by the back lanes, pulled the shears out of his neck and stuck in a knife from the bench. I had on a pair of rubber gloves. I missed the earring—never saw it.

'Then, on the way out, I dug up the blue roses—or what I thought were the blue roses—and pushed them into the back of the Land-Rover. I reckoned the swine owed me anything I could take. And that's what I took. My business is rocky. The blue roses would re-establish it for life. Nobody knew I was there—or so I thought. I knew where the blue roses were supposed to be, because Bell had showed me—showed me one in bloom, when he asked me to take them for budding on.'

'And the earring?'

'Sally never even told me of it. I believe she really thought she might have dropped it in the cottage, when we went for drinks in the evening. She couldn't have faced going back to the greenhouse to look for it. I had sufficient job getting her to go to the cottage that evening for drinks. But we had to. Bell's body was going to be found. It might look fishy if we hadn't turned up. She took a big dose of her calmative pills before she could make it. Next day, an awful reaction . . . She never told me about the earring. I didn't know she'd gone to the cottage on Monday, when . . . when . . .'

Wake motioned to Kippis, who took Clifford by the arm and led him gently through the garden door towards the road in front of the house, where Henderson and Tapp had already been loaded into an ambulance, and a police car waited.

Kate went over impulsively to Roger Wake. 'How can you possibly charge him, after all that? What good does it do?'

'Accessory after the fact of murder, Mrs Theobald,' Wake replied sadly. 'How can I possibly not charge him? But don't feel too bad. He'll plead guilty. And then— ask your husband—he may not even get prison, or, at least, only a token sentence.

Henry started towards the lane at the back, to his car.

'I must go and head off Sir Gerald,' he told Jonathan. 'I'll drop you off after.'

'I'm coming too,' declared Kate, clinging to him. 'Not for one moment are you to leave me—not today, any-how.'

When they turned into Pinchback lane, they saw a car parked outside Sir Gerald's farmhouse. Emerging from the gate was Dr McKay.

'Mamie Barrington is with Rosa,' he told them abruptly. 'I've phoned for Dick Vernon. He'll be round immediately, as soon as he gets instructions from his superiors.'

'What on earth?' asked Henry.

'Don't you know? I thought you must have been sent for, because of the note.'

'I haven't the slightest idea what this is about.'

'Sir Gerald. In his greenhouse.'

'How do you mean, in his greenhouse? You mean—dead?'

'Killed himself. There's no doubt about it. He slashed his wrists with a grafting knife—sharp as a razor. The note is addressed to you, Theobald. It's on the greenhouse bench. Better not touch it until the police get here.'

But Henry was already on his way towards the back of the house, with Kate and Jonathan following.

'I've covered him with a sheet,' called Dr McKay after them. 'Don't touch it.'

Kate stayed outside the greenhouse. Henry went in as briefly as he could, to get the note, trying not to look at the shape of the sheet on the floor.

The note was simple : 'Sorry, my dear fellow. I simply haven't the courage to face it.'

Kate was sniffing the air. 'Something's burning.'

Henry hastened to the back end of the garden.

On the little bonfire, where the paraffin had not quite soaked, straggled a few root ends of the roses.